A Tangle in Tenerife

A Sanford 3rd Age Club Mystery (#20)

David W Robinson

www.darkstroke.com

Copyright © 2020 by David W Robinson
Cover Photography by Adobe Stock © DiViArts
Design by soqoqo
All rights reserved.

No part of this book may be used or reproduced in any manner whatsoever without written permission of the author or Crooked Cat/darkstroke except for brief quotations used for promotion or in reviews. This is a work of fiction. Names, characters, and incidents are used fictitiously.

First Dark Edition, darkstroke, Crooked Cat Books 2020

Discover us online:
www.darkstroke.com

Find us on instagram:
www.instagram.com/darkstrokebooks

Include **#darkstroke** in a photo of yourself
holding this book on Instagram and
something nice will happen.

About the Author

David Robinson is a Yorkshireman now living in Manchester. Driven by a huge, cynical sense of humour, he's been a writer for over thirty years having begun with magazine articles before moving on to novels and TV scripts.

He has little to do with his life other than write, as a consequence of which his output is prodigious. Thankfully most of it is never seen by the great reading public of the world.

He has worked closely with Crooked Cat Books and darkstroke since 2012, when The Filey Connection, the very first Sanford 3rd Age Club Mystery, was published.

Describing himself as the Doyen of Domestic Disasters he can be found blogging at **www.dwrob.com** and he appears frequently on video (written, produced and starring himself) dispensing his mocking humour at **www.youtube.com/user/Dwrob96/videos**

The STAC Mystery series:

#1 The Filey Connection
#2 The I-Spy Murders
#3 A Halloween Homicide
#4 A Murder for Christmas
#5 Murder at the Murder Mystery Weekend
#6 My Deadly Valentine
#7 The Chocolate Egg Murders
#8 The Summer Wedding Murder
#9 Costa del Murder
#10 Christmas Crackers
#11 Death in Distribution
#12 A Killing in the Family
#13 A Theatrical Murder
#14 Trial by Fire
#15 Peril in Palmanova
#16 The Squire's Lodge Murders
#17 Murder at the Treasure Hunt
#18 A Cornish Killing
#19 Merry Murders Everyonee

Tales from the Lazy Luncheonette Casebook

#20 A Tangle in Tenerife

By the same author:

#1 A Case of Missing on Midthorpe
#2 A Case of Bloodshed in Benidorm

#1 The Anagramist
#2 The Frame

A Tangle in Tenerife

A Sanford 3rd Age Club Mystery (#20)

Chapter One

"Can things possibly get any worse?"

Joe Murray rooted through his backpack again, dragging out his laptop, a paperback, a couple of magazines, notebook and pen, and his tobacco tin and papers, frantically searching the lower depths of the bag.

"It wasn't in there, Joe," Sheila Riley told him. "I saw it in one of the side pockets."

Joe's eye blazed at her. "I'm just making sure. You'll let me do that, won't you? Before I lose the plot totally?"

His raised voice caused many heads to turn, amongst them two police officers who had been chatting with a pair of airport security people.

Sheila shushed him. "Keep your voice down. You're attracting attention."

"I've already attracted someone's attention, haven't I? Some thieving—"

Brenda Jump cut in, her voice not much above a whisper. "Be careful, Joe. Those police people are listening."

The four-handed law-enforcement-cum-security team were already moving around the crowded seating area towards them, but Joe remained unrepentant.

"I don't care who's listening. I've been robbed."

He had been in a bad mood for the last three hours: ever since he got to the Miner's Arms.

Recently re-elected as Chair of the Sanford Third Age Club, it was his task, along with Sheila as Membership Secretary and Brenda as the Treasurer, to organise outings for the 300-strong membership, and the earliest he could ever remember the coach departing the Miner's, was 7 a.m. That was for a trip to London.

When the three suggested a week in the Canary Islands as

a kind of convalescent break for Sheila, enough people were interested for Joe to open negotiations with the travel companies. It was something of a disappointment when only thirty or so members actually signed up to the deal, leaving him unable to negotiate better discounts than the one he eventually secured, but worse than the cost, they had to fly from Manchester Airport, not Leeds and Bradford, and their flight was scheduled out of Ringway at seven fifteen in the morning. By turn, that meant checking-in no later than quarter past five, and even at that hour, the journey from Sanford to South Manchester would take anything up to ninety minutes. Eventually, they left the car park of the Miners Arms a little after three in the morning, but to get there, Joe (and most of the members) had crawled out of bed at two. Some – amongst them, George Robson, Owen Frickley and the Staineses – had not even bothered going to bed.

"I managed an hour's sleep on the settee," Alec Staines told Joe when they boarded the bus in Sanford.

It had been a topsy-turvy winter. January proved cold and damp, but without any serious snow, which then arrived after a balmy, spring-like February. The cold snap returned in March, and it was only with the end of the month approaching, that the ice had given way to strong winds and persistent rain. Sharing a taxi to the Miners Arms with Sheila and Brenda, Joe confessed he would be glad to get on the plane, never mind land in Tenerife.

"At least we won't be affected by the weather."

When they boarded the bus, they found everyone in the same mood: grumpy. It was difficult for the potential excitement of a week in the Canary Islands to permeate the rain and general misery of a Manchester March.

Keith Lowry, the long-suffering driver from Sanford Coach Services, who regularly chauffeured the STAC members on their outings, made his feelings plain, and they were not much different to those of his passengers. "Why can't you people get on a plane at a sensible hour?"

Joe didn't argue. He couldn't. He felt the same way and

throughout the one and a quarter hour journey from Sanford to Manchester Airport, he kept up a string of grumbles at the unearthly hour the airline had compelled them to get moving.

Keith also complained that they had to go to Manchester for a flight. "What's wrong with Leeds and Bradford or Doncaster?"

"That was the deal," Brenda replied on Joe's behalf. "The best we could get."

Even though he had been the prime negotiator during the days of haggling with travel agents, grinding the price down as low as he could, Joe nevertheless felt hard done by, and he was further irritated by the prospect of a four and half hour flight without the option of a cigarette. Back in the days when he and his ex-wife had flown to the Costa Brava for their honeymoon, smokers were allocated seats to the rear of the aircraft. Now there wasn't even an option. In common with everywhere else, smoking was banned on all aircraft, and in the airport.

"I don't know what this country's come to," he whined when he got off the bus and stood outside the terminal building enjoying a cigarette to stoke up his nicotine levels.

Brenda stood with him while Sheila ensured that the members of their party had their flight tickets and collected their luggage from the bus. "It's called public health, Joe, and it's been that way for nigh on fifteen years." She indicated his hand-rolled cigarette. "That is a disgusting habit, and neither of us can work out why you started again after going all that time without.

"Blame Denise... RIP" Joe crossed himself. "And that silly mare chasing me in Palmanova. It was just too much to take. The tobacco eases my stress levels." His irritation rose again. "Hell, I can't even smoke in my own café these days. It's like living in a police state."

Sheila tried to mollify him. "You've never been able to smoke there. Not behind the counter, anyway. It's because it happens to be a café. The customers come in for food and drink, not to take in a passive cloud of toxins."

It was as if he were not listening to either of them. "You

can't smoke on the bus, can't smoke in the cinema, you can't even smoke in the pub anymore. What the hell is this country coming to?"

"Yes, Joe," Brenda said as Sheila ticked off the last members to leave the bus.

"You're just agreeing with me for the sake of agreeing with me."

"Yes, Joe."

Stubbing out his cigarette, taking out his tobacco and rolling another, Joe watched the STAC party trundling into the building. They were the usual suspects, he thought, but the poor weather and early morning departure had robbed them of their customary good cheer. Captain Les Tanner, normally dressed in regimental blazer, crisp white shirt, and tie, wore a heavy, quilted coat in black, and a flat cap not unlike Joe's. For once Tanner looked his age, and so too did his long-time girlfriend, Sylvia Goodson. Her eyes were heavy with lack of sleep, and her movements were more of a trudge than a ladylike stride. The Staines, Alec and Julia, were half asleep as they dragged their two small suitcases into the terminal, George Robson, Owen Frickley and Cyril Peck were muttering at each other, and the usually effusive Mavis Barker had to be woken to get off the bus.

Overhead, the Manchester skies were the same mutinous grey as those of West Yorkshire; cold and damp, threatening more rain. To Joe's tired mind, it seemed impossible that by early afternoon they would be basking in subtropical sunshine.

With his nicotine levels fully fuelled, he stepped into the airport and after checking in and going through security, he was even more outraged at the cost of a cup of tea and toast in one of the cafeterias.

"If I charged those prices, my customers would lynch me," he barked at the attendant.

Sheila was more upbeat. "If you charged those prices we'd be flying to the Bahamas not the Canaries."

Brenda supported her best friend. "All out of our profit share."

Joe valued friendship, and the members of the Sanford Third Age Club were his true friends. Only they could pass comments like that and do so with affection. Anyone else would receive a blast of frank opinion by return.

Joe's grumpiness was legendary throughout the town of Sanford. And he made no apology for it. He worked hard for his living, paid his rates and taxes on time and as far as he was concerned, that gave him an absolute right to complain when things were not as he believed they should be; even if that was only grumbling about the smoking ban and the mud dragged into his café on some trucker's boots.

After the unsatisfactory meal, Joe ambled around the busy departure lounge and shopping concourse, nodding to his members as he came across them, taking snaps of aircraft through the panoramic windows, and enjoying one of his favourite pastimes; people watching. A young family, the children restless and bored, mother and father tired, a couple in their thirties trying to sort out what looked like several passports, a few teenagers carrying rucksacks similar to his own.

He kept bumping into Les Tanner who was also taking photographs of aircraft through the windows. Eventually, leaving his bag with the two women, he made his way to the smoke area, situated above the shopping concourse and in a fenced off exterior zone from where he could watch ground crew preparing aircraft for their day's work.

But his irritation reached explosive levels when he came back and discovered that his compact camera had been stolen.

Sheila, her face flushed with embarrassment, was effusively apologetic. "It was there one moment, Joe, sticking out of the side pocket of your rucksack, and the next minute, the bag was still here but the camera was gone. I'm sorry."

Joe was furious, but stood before him, Sheila was near to tears and alongside her, Brenda looked just as unhappy.

He was tempted to vent his anger on his friends, but Sheila had undergone some of the worst months of her life since the previous Christmas, and he could not do it. Instead, he took it out on their surroundings.

"If they had the faintest idea about security, it wouldn't happen," he grumbled as the police and their security counterparts drew near.

"Is there some problem, sir?" asked the elder of the two police officers.

Joe translated 'sir' as 'sunbeam' and his annoyance rose accordingly. "Yes. My camera's been nicked."

"Well if you could just keep the noise down, sir—"

"Don't patronise me," Joe interrupted. "I'm playing hell. I have a right to play hell. I nipped out for a smoke, came back and I've been robbed. Do you know what that feels like?"

"We deal with it often enough, sir." The two men backed off to let the security officers take over.

Joe found the security woman sympathetic but unable to do much. "A Nikon Coolpix, Mr Murray?" she asked after taking his name, address, flight number and details of the camera.

"Easy to spot," Joe told her. "It has the initials LL scratched into the casing."

Her chubby, lugubrious face took on a new aura of suspicion. "LL? You said your name was Murray?"

"LL stands for Lazy Luncheonette." Joe watched her make a note of it. "It's a café. My business." He dipped into his brown leather wallet and took out a business card.

The security officer looked it over, made a note in her pocketbook, and attached the card to it. "We'll keep an eye out for it, sir. If we find it, we'll let you know. In the meantime, you are the best guardian of your own property. You should keep it with you, or make sure your friends are looking after it at all times."

Joe cast a mean glance at his companions. "Yeah. I'll do that."

With the departure of the security people, Brenda collected cups of tea for them while Sheila made an effort to make amends.

"We'll buy you a new camera. I feel so responsible for this. I should have been watching. I'm really sorry, Joe."

Again, he found it impossible to be angry, and moved to reassure her. "Stop worrying about it. And you will not buy me a new camera."

"What will you do for one? You always take lots of pictures when we go away."

"I have my Sony in the suitcase."

Brenda tutted. "Why all the fuss, then?"

Joe took a wax cup from her and quickly put it down at his feet, then blew on his fingertips.

Brenda handed a cup to Sheila. "Careful, Sheila, it's hot."

Joe took the opportunity to grumble further. "I notice you didn't warn me."

Brenda grinned slyly. "A man with your vast experience of catering, I thought you would have guessed." She sat alongside him, hemming him in between herself and Sheila. After clicking a couple of saccharin tablets into her cup and stirring it, she sipped approvingly. "So, like I said, if you've got another camera in your case, why are you making such a fuss over that old thing?"

"Precisely because it was an old thing." Joe removed the lid from his tea, dropped two sugars in and stirred it. "I've had that camera about three years, now. It was a compact. The Sony is good, but it's cumbersome. I have to faff about fitting the lenses and stuff. The Nikon was point and click." He waved at the crowded departure lounge. "Perfect for when you're hanging around places like this with nothing better to do."

Brenda checked her watch and then looked up at the flight information monitors. "We won't be hanging around much longer. They're calling us to the gate."

Joe sipped his tea again. "They can bloody well wait. This tea's too hot to drink that fast."

Sheila appeared relieved by the spirit in which he was now dealing with the theft. "Is this another one for the Joe Murray casebook? The case of the missing camera?"

"It could be," Brenda said. "I mean, no self-respecting thief would pinch anything that old, would they?"

"Right, so you think there was ulterior motive for taking it, do you?" Joe slurped more tea with a grimace of distaste. "Maybe it was MI5, huh? Maybe they thought I'd be selling pictures of the cafeteria prices to the Russians."

Brenda teased him further. "Maybe you inadvertently caught the pilot and one of the stewardesses in a compromising position," Brenda teased.

Sheila smiled wanly. "Really, Brenda. On the ground?"

"Stranger things have happened," Brenda rambled. "When we went to Australia, Colin was propositioned by a woman who wanted to join the Mile High—"

Joe cut off the inevitable naughty story. "They're not called stewardesses anymore. In this politically correct day and age, they're flight attendants." Putting down his cup, he went on, "Listen, I'm going for a last smoke before we get on the plane. Look out for my bag, will you? And this time, keep your flaming eyes on it."

"Yes, sir."

"Very good, sir." Sheila saluted.

Chapter Two

Ignoring their sarcasm, Joe hurried up the stairs and through the upper cafeteria, making for the outside smoking area.

He blamed himself for the stolen camera. He should have kept it in his pocket, or at the very least put it inside the backpack rather than in one of the side pockets.

He reasoned that the thief must have been an expert. Sheila and Brenda were notoriously sharp-eyed when it came to looking after their joint possessions, and any opportunist thief must have moved with all the speed and skill of a stage conjuror to spirit the camera away without the two women noticing.

Sheila's reaction was interesting. Given the disaster which had become her life over the last half year, he could reasonably expect her to break down in the face of such a crime, testing her already shaky resilience. And yet, she had not. Instead, she accepted culpability, even though Joe exonerated them both, and she did so with all the complex mixture of severity and efficiency compounded with apology that was her hallmark.

The previous Christmas and New Year had been difficult. Joe excused her from work at The Lazy Luncheonette, but she insisted on turning out with the rest of the team. From her point of view, it was better than sitting around the house dwelling on what might have been and what had happened. News of Martin Naylor's actions spread quickly through the town, and everyone, including the draymen of Sanford Breweries, treated her with kid gloves, an unaccustomed gentility wholly opposed to the usual ribaldry in The Lazy Luncheonette.

By the end of January, into early February, it was as if

nothing had ever happened, and even Brenda was surprised at their friend's recovery.

The coming week in Tenerife had originally been mooted as a means of aiding her recuperation, and Sheila was in total agreement from the moment it was suggested. It was all the more surprising because the origins of her problems lay in the Cape Verde Islands, fifteen hundred miles south of the Canaries. Yet, as the weeks and months progressed, her enthusiasm and anticipation grew as quickly as his and Brenda's.

He stepped out into the official smoking area, and the cold of the day hit him like an electric shock.

The sun had risen thirty minutes previously, but lay hidden behind the welter of turbulent cloud enveloping Manchester like a shroud. Such trivia did nothing to dissuade the hardened smokers crowding the small area, some of them, like Joe, clad in the kind of subtropical clothing they would need at their various destinations.

The smoke area was sealed off by a mesh grille, beyond which was a 30-foot drop to the airside. Under the bright lights, ground crew, wrapped up against the appalling weather worked on the airliners. Baggage trains and fuel tankers moved here and there, engineers, standing out in their quilted, high-visibility jackets, checked engine cowlings, fuselages or landing gear, and the air sang with the low whine of turbofans spooling up or winding down.

"It's like a miniature city."

He half turned to find a young man alongside him. It took a few moments to place him, but Joe recognised him from the airport as one half of the couple who had been organising their passports in the departure lounge.

Joe guessed him to be in his late thirties, a good few inches taller than himself. Fresh faced, pale-skinned with a head of neatly trimmed dark hair, there was a sadness about his brown eyes that activated Joe's agile mind.

He ignored the other's comment on the airport activity, and asked, "You don't enjoy flying?"

It took a second or two for the youngster to realise Joe was speaking to him. "What? Oh. Sorry. See what you mean. No. It doesn't worry me."

"It's just that you look a little, I dunno, cheesed off."

The young man smiled. "Cheesed off? Odd expression. Where did you get it from? An old episode of Dad's Army?"

Joe laughed grudgingly. "It was a common saying when I was your age." He offered his hand. "Joe Murray. From Sanford. West Yorkshire."

The younger man shook hands. "Rodney Wade. My friends call me Spike. I'm from Burnley… well, the Burnley area. A little village you've probably never heard of. Fence."

"You're right. I've never heard of it." Joe winked. "So, where are you going? Somewhere young and exciting?"

"Tenerife."

Joe's smile broadened. "Snap. First time there?"

Spike shook his head. "For Tabby, yes, but I've been there plenty of times."

"Tabby?"

"My wife, Tabitha. She prefers Greece. Well, she did classical studies at university, and she knows all the legends of Greek mythology. But this is a belated honeymoon and Tabby wanted to try the Canaries, so here we are. How about you? Been to Tenerife before?"

"A long time ago." He did not think Spike would be interested in the tale of his escape from Palmanova. Thoughts of the young man's name brought a frown to his forehead. "Your friends call you Spike? Why, for God's sake?"

Spike shrugged and crushed out his cigarette. "Just one of those things. I had spiky hair when I was at school, and the nickname stuck with me."

Mavis Barker put out her cigarette and squeezed past Joe. "Stoked up for the flight, Joe."

Joe smiled back. "Good on you, Mavis." He found Spike smiling, too. "She's one of my crowd. Thirty of us altogether."

"OAP holiday, is it?"

"Cheeky sod." Joe laughed. "Mind you, you're not far off. The Sanford 3rd Age Club. We're not all pensioners, but those who aren't are getting there fast." More soberly, he went on, "Normally, we enjoy weekends away, but the weather's been so bad, the gang felt like something different."

As explanations went, it was easier than the more intricate truth.

"So where are you staying?" Spike asked.

Joe frowned again. "I think it's called the Torviscas Atoll. Something like that."

"Snap. So are Tabby and me."

The word snap reminded Joe of his camera. "I saw you in the departure lounge. I was wandering around taking pictures of the aeroplanes and I noticed you sorting your passports out."

Spike's clear brow creased. "You can't be too careful, you know. I keep telling Tabby, keep the passports safe. She complains when I ask to see them, but I'm just making sure she has them safely tucked away. Especially in a busy place like an airport. You know what I mean?"

Joe snorted. "Do I ever? Someone stole my camera while we were hanging round back there." He shuddered at the irritating memory.

"Oh, that was you?"

"Yeah. Not my day, you probably saw me arguing with the cops and security." Seeing that Spike was not particularly interested, Joe changed the subject. "So, if you're at the Atoll, maybe we'll see you around, huh?"

"Maybe you will."

Congratulating himself on his ability to make new friends despite his reputation for surliness, Joe crushed out his cigarette, and with a final, "See you," made his way back into the terminal where he found his two companions urgently checking their watches.

Sheila scolded him. "Everyone's making for the gate. We thought you weren't going to make it."

"You worry too much. Which way do we go?"

Brenda handed Joe his backpack, and picked up her handbag. "Follow me. And make sure you've got your boarding pass."

While he made his way behind the two women and other passengers along the spur leading away from the departure lounge, Joe found Les Tanner alongside him.

"Lost your camera, I believe, Murray?" As always, Tanner's tones were clipped, military, befitting a man who was in charge of a small department at Sanford town Hall, and who had been an officer in the Territorial Army.

Joe had learned to disregard the authoritarian air many years previously, but there were still times when it irked. "Do you make a speciality of getting up my nose, Les?"

"I could," Tanner agreed, "but I can find better things to do with my life. It simply occurred to me that losing your camera is entirely symptomatic of your lackadaisical approach to everything."

"And you could do so much better?" Joe stopped and stared his antagonist in the eye. "Remind me who misplaced his camera in Cornwall last year—"

"It was stolen, not lost."

"— And who got it back for him."

"Only after the police were finished with it."

"Let me tell you something Les. I didn't lose the damn camera. Someone stole it. And I won't be here to find it for myself. Now come on. We're supposed to be on holiday, aren't we? Call a truce for the coming week." Joe walked on, hurrying to catch up with Sheila and Brenda.

When they reached the far end, it was to find most of the available seating already taken. Joe saw Spike Wade sat by the windows, along with his wife clutching their passports. George Robson and Owen Frickley were chatting with Alec and Julia Staines, while Mavis Barker had nodded off to sleep again.

Through the large windows, a telescopic bridge projected from the building to the forward door of their aircraft. Joe could see the pilot and co-pilot in the cockpit, chatting, laughing over something.

"How do they stay up?" Brenda asked. "The aeroplane, I mean, not the crew."

Joe had the answer "Speed. The forward momentum and fast moving air under the wings, lifts it off the ground. As long as it's moving forward, it'll stay aloft."

Brenda grinned. "You're a mine of useless information, aren't you, dear?"

"Yes, but there's one piece of information I'm short of right now."

Brenda raised her eyebrows and Joe snorted.

"Where's my cam…"

He trailed off on seeing the security guard he'd dealt with earlier, hurrying towards them.

"Mr Murray," she gasped, almost out of breath by the time she reached them. "We… we think we've got… got your camera."

She handed the item over and Joe checked it. On the battery compartment he made out the scratched initials LL. "Yes. It's mine."

With a broad smile, the security officer produced a form. Joe checked the details and signed it. While she walked off and the passengers began to move to the gate, Joe switched the camera on, and checked the photographs he had taken earlier.

"That just about makes my day."

"What's wrong, Joe?" Sheila asked. "You got it back, didn't you?"

He showed her the blank screen on the rear of the camera, and its simple message. *No image.*

"Now why would anyone go the trouble of stealing my camera just to wipe the images off it?"

Chapter Three

"Good morning, ladies and gentlemen, this is Captain Dorrans, and I'd like to welcome you aboard flight 773 from Manchester to Tenerife. We're currently cruising at thirty-nine thousand feet, out over the Irish Sea. We'll turn south over Dublin and from there it's a nice straight line down to the Canary Islands. The weather in Tenerife is sunny, the temperature is forecast for a very warm twenty-five degrees. We took off on schedule and we anticipate being on the ground at about twelve noon local time. I'll keep you updated at intervals during the flight, in the meantime relax, enjoy the flight, and if there's anything you need, just ask the cabin staff."

In the aisle seat of row six, on the right hand side of the aircraft, Joe closed his paperback copy of le Carre's *Smiley's People* and snorted. "Relax? How are you supposed to relax when you're crammed into a pressurised cigar tube and you can't even have a smoke?"

Alongside him, in the centre of the three seats, Sheila let the in-flight magazine fall into her lap. "I never realised you were a nervous flyer, Joe."

"We had this debate when we went to Torremolinos and Majorca. I am not nervous, I am not worried about flying. I am annoyed."

"Your photographs?"

He nodded. "What do you think?"

She brushed a rogue blonde hair from her eyes. "I just said what I think. You look nervous to me."

Joe grunted. "Yes, well, I'm not. I'm irritated. I can't have a smoke."

He glanced to his left, across the aisle and through one of

the windows slightly ahead of their position, where he could see a blaze of morning sunshine. What a change from a drab and dreary West Yorkshire five hours earlier.

If the return of the camera lifted his spirits, albeit only slightly, it did more for Sheila and Brenda, appeasing their uneasy feelings of guilt and allowing them to drop back into their more comfortable roles of teasing their friend and boss.

The morning sun burst through the left hand windows, and welcome though it was, it did little to dampen Joe's annoyance. Barely forty minutes into the flight, he already wanted another cigarette. Forty minutes! Working in his café he could go anything up to two hours between cigarettes. Why was he so desperate for one now?

Boredom. That was the simple answer. Life at The Lazy Luncheonette was anything but boring. He opened his doors at six every morning and from seven o'clock, when the draymen from Sanford Breweries began to turn up in need of breakfast, it was non-stop. He didn't have time to think about smoking, let alone actually squeeze a cigarette in. Sat on this airborne bus, he had nothing to do other than read, and with reading came the need for a smoke.

He tried to calm his annoyance with the thought that at least they were airborne and in just over four hours, they would be stepping out into glorious sunshine and temperatures that were often no more than a dream in Great Britain. But it did not work. He was still angry, still bored, still in need of a nicotine fix.

"Do you know where Alison lives?"

Sheila's question snapped him from his reverie. He and Alison had been divorced a long time, and the last Joe saw her was when he fled to Tenerife after the events in Palmanova.

"I stayed with her for a while if you remember," he replied to Sheila's question. "And back then she was working in a pub across the road from where we're staying."

"Sounds like Joe has his own agenda," Brenda commented with a gaping yawn.

"Doesn't it just?" Sheila's reply was vague, and her

friends noticed she had one eye on the flight attendant stocking up her trolley by the forward galley.

Brenda followed Sheila's gaze. "Goody. Brekkers. I'm starving."

Joe huffed out his breath. "You already had breakfast at the airport. How can you be hungry?"

"I'm a growing girl." Brenda grinned slyly and changed the subject. "Remind me, Joe, what prompted Ali to go to Tenerife in the first place?"

The question took Joe by surprise. He was certain both women knew the answer. "She said she'd just had enough of England, and she'd found work in the Canaries selling holiday apartments or something."

"Timeshare?" Sheila asked.

"Something like that. You'd have to ask her about that. Anyway, about a year later it went base over apex and Ali now works behind the bar of The Mother's Ruin. That's the pub I was telling you about. Right across the road from our hotel."

The breakfast trolley was out of the galley and making its way along the aisle. All three lowered their seat trays. Joe noticed that Brenda had the most difficulty letting it all the way down.

"Bloody aeroplanes," she grumbled. "Never enough room."

"A growing girl, huh?" Joe laid a mean eye on her generous midriff. "You sure you haven't got a little something growing in there that you haven't told us about?"

Brenda sniffed disdainfully. "Chance would be a fine thing." The cheeky grin returned to her face. "I may have that problem on the way back. If I get lucky."

Joe scowled and Sheila laughed aloud. "If Brenda can't get a little loving in the Canary Islands, where can she?"

"As long as she's not asking me to provide the loving," Joe muttered and pressed himself back into his seat as the flight attendant passed breakfast over to Brenda and then Sheila.

His last remark was at the least disingenuous. He and

Brenda had been spending the occasional night together since just before the previous Christmas. It had been that way on and off for many years. They were the best of friends, but romance was never a factor. It was, Joe reflected, sex, nothing more. The need to relieve the infrequent pressure of their libidos, and both of them were happy with the situation.

Lowering his seat tray, he took his breakfast from the flight attendant and peeled open the microwaved container. His eyes fell in dismay on the contents.

"What is this?"

"A hash brown, sir," said the flight attendant.

"I didn't mean the hash brown, I mean the whole thing. I run a proper café, you know, in Sanford. If I served the brewery drivers something like this they'd have me shot. There isn't enough here to feed Brenda's cat."

"I'm sorry about that, sir." The young woman passed him a wax cup full of tea. "We would have some difficulty getting the ovens and hobs on board, and you'd never believe how long the kettle takes to boil on two car batteries."

Joe ignored her sarcasm. He chewed and swallowed a Frankfurter sausage. "And these hash browns should be black puddings."

"I'll mention it in my report, sir. Now, if there's nothing else, I must get on."

Sheila silently scolded him with a glare. Brenda was more up front. "You really are the pits sometimes, Joe. Airline food has never been the best, and you know it."

Joe speared a hash brown with his plastic fork. "And if no one complains they'll never improve, will they?"

Sheila switched to begging. "Could we please stop grumbling? We're going away to enjoy a week of sun and seaside." She pushed her breakfast away and drank a mouthful of tea. "I'm looking forward to it. After the debacle over Christmas, and the freezing weather this last month, we deserve a bit of sun and sand."

Brenda grinned. "You forgot the sex."

Deliberately avoiding the provocative remark, Joe munched on a small piece of stringy bacon and swallowed it.

It was Sheila's first reference to the events of the previous Christmas, which almost took her life, and he was uncertain how to respond. A quick glance in Brenda's direction told him that she felt the same way.

Sheila did not rise to Brenda's remark. "The only thing that concerns me with Tenerife is, are we going to see another murder?"

"After sex." Finished with the unsatisfactory meal, Brenda, too, pushed it away and swallowed a mouthful of tea.

"What is it with you and sex?" Joe asked. "Are you going to keep coal in them?"

Brenda frowned and Sheila laughed. "It's an old joke, Brenda. Mother always used to say that sex was what posh people kept coal in."

"If you think I keep coal in—"

Joe interrupted her. "There's nothing like a good murder to spice up a holiday."

"And sex," Brenda said.

Sheila changed the subject yet again. "So, Joe, you got your camera back, why so annoyed."

He paused with a plastic fork full of baked bins midway between his tray and mouth, his eyes vacant, staring straight ahead at the bulkhead behind which the cabin crew carried out their work.

Putting the fork down in the tray, he said, "I spent ages wandering round the departure lounge taking pictures, and you know how I enjoy taking pictures."

Brenda confirmed it. "After making money and solving a good murder, it's your favourite pastime."

"Yeah, well, then someone nicked the camera and wiped the pictures from it. Why?"

Brenda collected the detritus of her meal and jammed it all into the tray. Taking a mouthful of tea and grimacing, she said, "Worse than the tea at The Lazy Luncheonette." Placing the lid back on her cup, she went on, "Maybe they looked at the pictures and thought you were a crap photographer." She grinned at his scowl.

"And maybe the altitude is getting at that excuse you call a brain." Joe paused to let the gibe sink in. "I'm being serious here. That camera is about five years old. It's worth maybe twenty quid on E-bay. If someone is gonna nick it, fine. If they're then gonna chuck it away, fine. But why erase the images and then let me get it back? It doesn't make sense."

Sheila too finished the unsatisfactory meal and tucked everything into the tray awaiting collection. Her features a mask of deep thought, she said, "Unless you inadvertently took a photograph someone didn't want you to have."

Brenda laughed, drawing the sharp, disapproving attention of Les Tanner across the aisle. She pulled her tongue out at him, then said to Sheila, "You're getting as suspicious and paranoid as Joe."

Her best friend rose to the challenge. "Can you explain it?"

"As a matter of fact, I think Sheila is right," Joe intervened before an argument could break out. The two women, known locally as Joe's Harem, were the best of friends, but they did have the occasional spat.

"Go on."

"I took a lot of pictures of the aeroplanes through the windows, and some of the departure lounge. Maybe I snapped someone in the lounge who wasn't supposed to be there."

Brenda cackled again. "A lovers' tryst. Maybe it was Elvis alive and well and living in *Coronation Street*. You're potty, the both of you. Joe, someone half-inched your camera, took the memory card out of it, kept that and chucked the rest away."

Joe smiled a smile of superior knowledge. "Nice idea, Brenda, but for one thing."

"What?"

"I don't use a memory card in this camera. It's a compact, remember. I don't use it as much as the Sony, and its internal memory is big enough for the few pictures I take with it."

***

"This is Captain Dorrans again. We're about to go into our descent, and thanks to our friends in Air Traffic Control, we'll be slightly ahead of schedule when we touch down in about twenty minutes. On behalf of myself and my crew, I hope you've enjoyed your flight, and that you have a wonderful and relaxing holiday."

Alongside Joe, his companions began to gather their possessions and stow them for landing. Following their lead, Joe dropped his paperback in his bag, and unfastened his seat belt. "I'd better go to the smallest room again before we land."

"Too many beers," Sheila commented.

"Baby beer." As he said it, he realised that he had lost count of the number of small cans of lager he had consumed.

There was a queue for the toilets at the front. Joe looked over his shoulder, to the rear of the cabin, and learnt there was another queue for those facilities. He gripped the back of the seat ahead of him, hauled himself upright, stepped out into the aisle, and moved forward to join the shorter queue.

Joe tagged on behind a middle-aged man. Bushy eyebrows hid a solemn stare and a bulbous nose shone bright red in the glow of sunlight coming through the windows. He was a little taller than Joe's five feet six, a lot chubbier around the midriff and where Joe's curly mop floundered around his head, the other's balding pate was part hidden beneath a white, plant-pot hat.

Joe offered his hand. "Joe Murray."

The other shook it. "Harold Givens. From Burnley. Most people call me Harry."

"Better than some of the things people call me." Joe felt the soft-skinned palm, his mind slipping into analytical mode. Strong grip, soft skin; he was an office manager, or something of that ilk. The strength of his grip said he was determined, accustomed to being in control but the smoothness of the palm, said he did nothing physical. Harry Givens had never done a day's hard work in his life, or not what Joe Murray would call hard work.

"I have a friend who lives in the Burnley area. Just outside

Sabden. Sir Douglas Ballantyne. Maybe you've heard of him."

Givens laughed. "Show me anyone from that area who hasn't. You're from up our way, are you, Joe?"

"Nah. Sanford. West Yorkshire." When Givens appeared surprised, he explained, "Manchester was the nearest airport where we could get a flight today."

"Ah. Right. Just you and the missus?" Givens nodded towards Sheila.

This time, Joe's laugh was louder. "My missus went to Tenerife a good few years ago and never came back. No, I'm Chair of the Sanford 3rd Age Club. There are about thirty of us and we're staying at the Torviscas Atoll."

"The world gets even smaller," said Givens. "I'm staying at the same hotel. I always do. Have you been there before?"

Joe shook his head. "I'll be honest, Harry, these days, I'm more your Scarborough or Skegness kinda guy. I've been to the Canary Islands before." He shuddered at the recollection of his dash from Palmanova. In order to suppress it, he worked quickly through a montage of memories. "Come to that, I've been to many parts of the world, mostly in the days when I was married, and I've seen all I wanna see, but our club is a democracy and the members voted for it."

He could have added that it was his idea, but he did not.

"I like Tenerife." There was a hint of defiance in Givens' voice as if he were challenging Joe to disagree. "Warm all year round, without getting too hot, food's digestible and you get decent, English beer there."

"You could say the same about Skegness," Joe argued. "Except for the warm all year round bit."

Givens laughed, a low grunt like the snort of a pig. "I'd argue about the decent English beer in Skegness. Always said, you can't get a decent pint south of Knutsford."

Joe, too, laughed. "Sheffield on our side of the Pennines."

"Listen, Joe, do yourself a favour. There's a pub right across the road from the Atoll. The Mother's Ruin. Kenny, the lad who runs it, keeps a belting pint, and he has entertainment on every night. Music from the sixties right up to the nineties."

"I know it well," Joe declared. He was telling the truth this time. He had worked there as a short order cook during his stay on the island, while he was on the run from Palmanova. "My crowd will love it. The sixties, anyway. Not so sure about the nineties. Kenny, did you say? When I was last there it was a guy named Paddy McLintock who ran it."

"Sold up last year, mate. Ken Lowfield is the guy what owns it now."

"As long as the ale is up to snuff. Maybe I'll see you in there, Harry."

"Bound to. Listen, Joe, while you're there, make sure you take the all-island tour or the Teide tour. You may find the island tour a bit, I dunno, tiring. It's an all day job, you know. Teide is about six hours, and they bring you back via a perfume factory outlet at Guia de Isora. You'll pick up some real bargains for your girlfriends." Givens nodded at Sheila.

Joe was forced to laugh again. "Sheila and Brenda are not my girlfriends. They're my friends and they also work for me."

"Sorry. No wife, then?"

"I did have, but she moved a few years ago."

"Really? Somewhere better than Sanford?"

"I told you. Tenerife."

Five minutes later, with the aircraft banking hard left for the final approach, cabin crew hurrying along the aisle to check that seat belts were fastened, seats upright and trays locked away, Joe retook his seat and clipped his belt loosely across his lap.

"Been making friends?" Sheila asked.

"Harry Givens. He's from Lancashire, but he's a nice bloke for all that. Told me where you and Brenda can buy cheap perfume."

Brenda smiled broadly. "I like him already."

"Something worrying him, though," Joe said. "Has that look in his eye. You know what I mean? Everything is not right with the world."

"And as if that's not enough, he has to bump into you."

Sheila laughed at Brenda's comment. Joe scowled.

Chapter Four

San Eugenio lay northwest of Playa de Las Américas, a sprawl of holiday hotels and theme parks spread either side of Autopista TF-1.

Their courier, Diana, an energetic young woman with a head of neatly permed blonde hair, kept up a stream of chatter over the microphone during the 20-minute journey from the airport. After dropping other holidaymakers at various locations in and around Las Américas, the coach finally arrived at the Torviscas Atoll, on the upper corner of *Avenida de España*, where the road picked up the motorway again.

A large, low rise apartment complex composed of four-storey blocks of apartments, it dominated the skyline of the busy street. Opposite was The Mother's Ruin, the English pub Joe had told his two friends about, next door to which was an English chippy and two other bars. Alongside the Atoll's entrance was a small supermarket, and beneath the hotel's front facing block was a parade of shops and restaurants, greeters standing on the hot pavements, hoping to persuade passers-by into dining with them. Looking north, towards the motorway, several miles inland were the dramatic foothills of Mt Teide, and by looking up, past the nearer escarpments, they could see the peak of the volcano, a tiny cone sitting in the distance, its peak white with snow.

After the coach left its last but one port of call, the *Iberostar Bouganville Playa*, Joe was not surprised to find that the majority of the remaining passengers were the thirty or so STAC members, Spike Wade and his wife, a shapely brunette, and Harry Givens.

Spike introduced Joe to his wife, Tabby, and as he shook

hands, Joe detected a hint of sadness in the woman's brown eyes. A little younger than her husband, Joe guessed her to be somewhere in her mid-thirties. Pretty, with a well-tended figure, her hands were soft, her handshake flimsy, and unlike Spike, her skin, large amounts of which were on show, was white, as if she had not left British shores for some time.

"Friends or family?" asked Diana, the courier as the Wades went ahead of them into the hotel.

"I met him at Manchester Airport," Joe reported as his members began to file off the bus and collect their luggage. "Nice couple. From somewhere in Lancashire." He smiled at Diana. "You're not from the north of England?"

She giggled. "Maidenhead. Near Slough. A bit to the west of London. Haven't been home for a couple of years now. I prefer it here." She held her hands up to the clear skies and soaring temperatures. "Sun, sand, no rain... well, not much rain. Everything I want is on this island."

"My ex-wife lives here, and she feels the same way. You don't miss the old country?"

Diana shook her head. "What's to miss?"

Sheila and Brenda joined them, Brenda running a handkerchief over her brow. "Dear me, it's hot." She beamed on Diana. "Is Joe trying to charm your knickers off?"

Diana laughed again and Joe frowned at his companion. "Stop embarrassing the girl and help her get the old gits sorted out."

Brenda shook her head. "I'm not embarrassing her. I'm embarrassing you."

"Embarrassing Joe? Sheila smiled at Diana. "That is what's known as flogging a dead horse."

The driver flung luggage from his underslung racks onto the hot pavements, club members grabbed their cases and headed for the shade of the hotel lobby.

"You're the organiser, Mr Murray?" Diana asked as Joe took charge of his own bag.

"Please call me Joe. And yes, me, Sheila and Brenda are the lead names on the booking." He dragged the case toward the lobby. "I'd be grateful if you could make it clear to the management that problems can be addressed to any of us three."

"No problem, but you'll find that the managers and desk clerks all speak excellent English."

"Good job," said Brenda from ahead of them. "The only Spanish we ever learned was from *Fawlty Towers*."

Diana laughed again and entering the lobby, fought her way through the crowd to the reception counter where she spoke in rapid, fluent Spanish to the clerk. Throughout her chatter, she kept waving towards the door. After the brief exchange, she made her way back to the exit where Joe, Sheila and Brenda were bringing up the rear.

"I've spoken to Pablo. He's the Reception Manager, on day duty this week, and I've made him aware of your names. I'm the duty courier for this hotel, but I have other places where I have to be at certain times. I leave a notice up here in reception with the times I'm here on duty, and if you have any problems when I'm not here, this is my mobile number." She handed Joe a card. "Enjoy your holiday, and for those of you who want to attend, I'll be holding the formal reception round the pool at ten o'clock tomorrow morning."

"Thanks, Diana." Joe passed the card to Sheila.

"You're welcome. I'll catch you tomorrow."

Diana disappeared back out into the sunshine and the queue for reception began to shuffle forward.

Tagging onto the back end, Joe noticed the Wade couple making their way into the complex alongside Harry Givens.

"They're from the same area," Joe commented.

Sheila, who had been studying Diana's card, looked up. "Huh?"

Joe pointed to the threesome disappearing towards the sunshine of the poolside. "Harry Givens and the Wade kids. They're all from Burnley. At least that's what they told me."

"They'll be able to understand one another, then." Brenda delivered a gaping yawn. "Personally, I never could understand Lancastrians."

Joe tutted. "Not even a little Englander, but a little Yorkshire-er."

She grinned back. "No, Joe. I speak the international language of lurve." She swayed her hips at him. "Want some lessons?"

"Pass. Tell you what we do need, though: milk, sugar, water, teabags."

Sheila leapt at the suggestion. "You two stay in the queue while I nip to the supermarket next door."

"What'll we do if we never see her again?" Brenda whispered.

"Take her money, spend it and inform her sons that she's been sold into slavery." Joe frowned. "Tell you what; she's bearing up well, isn't she?"

"She always was a tough old bird, Joe. A lot tougher than you and me. Don't worry, I'll be keeping an eye on her."

"Almost four months now, and we'll both be keeping an eye on her, but if she's doing any crying, it's in private."

Notwithstanding the crowd, Pablo and his female assistant, Nina, worked quickly, taking passports, handing out electronic key cards to the rooms and in less than ten minutes, by the time Sheila returned from the supermarket, Nina was attending to the women while Pablo dealt with Joe.

Slightly overweight, balding, he was a jovial man who, as Diana had promised, spoke excellent English. "You are the famous Joe."

"Well, I'm Joe for sure."

"No, no, señor, you are famous all over Adeje." Pablo grinned. "You are private dick, and your old wife, she tells everyone of your adventures."

"Old wife? You make her sound like an antique. You mean ex-wife."

"This is so. Alis-on, she is well known in Adeje. And Diana tells me if we have problems, we should bring them to you."

"Depends on the problem."

Pablo laughed gregariously. "My girlfriend, I think she cheats on me. You prove it? Yes?" He roared with laughter again.

Joe tutted. "I think Diana means problems with our party."

He gestured at Sheila and Brenda. "If you have any trouble from our mob, speak to me or one of these two ladies. But you shouldn't have any serious issues with them. We're all too old for rioting and bed-hopping..." Joe glanced at Brenda. "Although there may be the odd exception to that rule."

Pablo grinned again. "There are times when we have more trouble with the older generation, Señor Joe. But they're easier to deal with, too." He slapped the back of his hand. "We give them a smack on the bottom and they behave." He took Joe's passport and handed over the card key. "You are in 401C. Block C, level four, room one." He pointed the way on a plan of the complex. "Past the pool, you'll find the lift, up to level four, turn left out of the lift, and it's on the end. Your lady friends and in 402, right next door." He winked at Joe. "Hey. No bed-hopping huh?"

Joe chuckled. "I'll try to keep it down."

"Not down, you need, señor, but..." Pablo trailed off under a steely glare from Sheila.

She made her feelings plain. "Men. Same the whole world over."

Dragging his suitcase along, Joe led the way through reception and out into sunlight at the rear where the pool area took up the greater part of available space. A large pool, shaped like an elongated peanut, with a sheltered bar to the nearer side.

"Tempting." Brenda smacked her lips as they passed along the sidewalk.

"What? The pool or the bar?" Sheila asked.

"Both. What do you think, Joe? Strip down to your cozzy, a quick dip then a swift half, or what?"

Joe was not listening. He was concentrating on the blocks around them. Forming a large triangle, which hemmed the pool in, every apartment had its own sunward, southerly facing balcony, but on the blocks to their immediate left the balconies were on the far side. Here they could see only the deck access terraces which ran along the block. Three flights up, Givens had stopped at his apartment. Spike Wade and his

30

wife were further along, and Spike had turned to face Givens. They were too far away for Joe to hear what they were saying, but there was no mistaking Spike's anger. He pointed a shaking finger at Givens who dismissed it with a two-fingered gesture.

"Something definitely wrong, there," Joe muttered, and fell in behind his two companions again.

While not up to the usual standards of luxury enjoyed by the Sanford 3rd Age Club, Joe found his apartment comfortable and spacious. Whenever they went on outings, many members shared rooms, but Joe preferred to be alone. He tended to stay up late and get up early, which would create problems for others, so life was simpler if he paid the single occupancy supplement. Apartment 401C was designed to sleep up to four people; twin beds in the single bedroom and two fold-out bed settees in the living room. There was a tiny kitchen, but Joe knew except for making the odd cup of tea, he would not need its facilities. There was a small dining table and four chairs in the living room, ideal for plugging in his laptop on which he would keep a journal for the week, and a plastic table with chairs out on the balcony. A TV stood silent on the cabinet. Joe refused to pay €20 to use it. He rarely watched TV at home.

Best of all was the balcony. When he stepped out onto it, he found himself instantly baking in the early afternoon sun. The view was exactly what he wanted; looking out over the tops of nearby hotels and apartment complexes, their swimming pools surrounded by sunbathers, out to the ocean half a mile away, and twenty miles further out lay the island of La Gomera, standing proud of the serene waters.

Closer to home he could see the gaily coloured chutes of men and woman parasailing, their speedboats cutting twin wakes in the water, and further out, plodding across the sparkling waters of the Atlantic, was the ferry from Los Christianos to La Gomera.

All at once, the hassles of the day receded; losing his camera, getting it back, finding the images removed, the tiresome four and a half hour flight, and the hour or more getting through Tenerife Airport and the bus ride to the Torviscas Atoll, drained from him, becoming a distant memory belonging to another life. A sense of peace and wellbeing came over him.

"This is what it's all about," he told himself.

"Joe."

Brenda's voice impinged upon his reverie. "Back to the land of the living." He looked to his left and there was the woman herself leaning on the balcony not ten feet from him.

The building was so arranged that each apartment was set back from the next one so that Joe had a view not only of Brenda and Sheila's balcony, but those of other apartments beyond them, and, when he looked down, the whole of the pool area and the other two blocks in the complex.

He concentrated on Brenda. "What?"

"We've got the kettle on. Come round and have a cup of tea."

"I haven't even unpacked, yet."

"You can do that later. We have tea and cake."

He tutted. "Let me just change and I'll be with you."

He ducked back into his apartment, passed through to the bedroom where he unlocked and opened his suitcase. He spent a few minutes hanging up shirts and jeans, stowing his socks and underwear, then casting off his northern English clothing, he dragged on a pair of denim shorts, and a short-sleeved shirt, and slipped his foot into a pair of pool loafers. Finally, putting on his fisherman's gilet, he dropped his wallet, tobacco, cigarette papers and lighter into the pockets, picked up his key and stepped out onto the rear deck access.

Four floors beneath him and thirty yards further back, traffic sped along Autopista TF-1. Across the other side of the motorway, he could see a huge fun park, but it looked closed, almost abandoned, and beyond it were more holiday complexes. Behind them were the foothills of Teide, and again, he could make out the cone of the volcano, small and insignificant from this distance, almost lost amongst the nearer hills and escarpments. It was hard to imagine that tiny peak dominating the island.

He rapped on the door of 402C and a moment later, Brenda opened it to let him in.

Already the apartment had the unmistakeable air of two women sharing. Dresses and coats hung on doors, travel clothes, discarded in favour of more tropical attire, were folded in neat piles on the settee and occasional table.

Sheila was already out on the balcony, a small pot of tea, sugar bowl and milk jug sitting in the centre, a plate containing a small fruitcake alongside them, and a third place set for their boss.

"I bought some milk, sugar, teabags and a bottle of water for you, Joe," Sheila told him.

"How much do I owe you?"

"Call it five Euros for cash."

He dipped into his wallet, handed the money over, and taking his seat, helped himself to a cup of tea, stirred in some milk and sugar and rolled a cigarette. "I've only been here ten minutes and I could get used to this."

"It is rather peaceful, isn't it?" Brenda helped herself to a slice of fruitcake.

Sheila popped her sunglasses on and stared at the street below and across to the parade where The Mother's Ruin stood on the corner. "What's that above the pub? Is it a tanning salon?"

Joe looked across and squinted his eyes against the glare of the sun. "Who'd need a tanning salon here? No, it's some kind of dance club."

Brenda cackled, and through a mouthful of cake said, "Yes. Lap dancing. You are a pair of short-sighted idiots, aren't you?"

Sheila blushed and Joe excused himself. "Sun's in my eyes." Lighting the cigarette he blew smoke out with a satisfied hiss, and looked at the balcony next door. "Who's in there? Do we know?"

"Alec and Julia Staines," Sheila said.

"Blinds drawn, door shut, must have decided to catch up on some sleep, huh?"

Brenda giggled again, swallowed her cake and washed it

down with a gulp of tea. "Cloud cuckoo land again. If I know Alec and Julia, they're catching up all right, but not on their sleep. Something just as horizontal, I'll bet."

Sheila giggled. "Brenda, you're incorrigible."

"I wouldn't know. I don't know what it means."

To distract them, Joe looked across the ocean. "Am I right in thinking that's La Gomera?" he asked.

Sheila nodded. "Fascinating place. They communicate by whistling to each other across the mountains and ravines."

Brenda chuckled again. "A bit like the dance halls in Sanford."

Ignoring her, Sheila went on with her lecture. "It's a language all of its own, called, I believe, Silbo Gomero. I remember this marvellous programme about it on Radio Four a few years back. The island is very hilly, but the whistling can be heard up to two miles away. It was a tradition that was dying out, but the local government have insisted it be taught in the schools."

Joe approved. "Well that makes for a pleasant change. The kids back home are coming out of school after years of being taught nothing. Not even good manners."

Sheila, a former school secretary, gave him her most disapproving stare. "That's unfair, Joe, and you know it. Branding all schoolchildren because of an unruly minority."

"Unruly? Feral, more like."

Joe brought his gaze closer to home and the Atoll's swimming pool. The Sanford 3rd Age Club members had wasted no time. George Robson and Owen Frickley were in swimming shorts, sunbathing on loungers. Nearby, Les Tanner was arranging a parasol to keep the direct sunlight off Sylvia Goodson, and Mavis Barker was at the bar with a tall glass in front of her. Even from this distance, without his sunglasses, Joe could see that the glass contained cola, but he knew Mavis too well. She preferred her cola watered down with Pernod or Bacardi.

As he watched, Spike and Tabby Wade walked around the pool, picked a couple of sun loungers and set them up close to George and Owen. They had barely got themselves comfortable when the shadow of Harry Givens fell over them.

Joe clucked. "The people on Gomera can hear whistling from a couple of miles, and I can't hear what's been said down there from fifty yards."

Opinions were obviously being exchanged. Spike raised his sunglasses and said something to Givens, who must have retorted, causing Spike to sit up. At that point, George Robson also sat up and spoke to them. George, a gardener for Sanford Borough Council was short but stocky, a muscular man, always ready to wade in with his fists if he had to.

Whatever the outcome, Givens pointed at Spike, then turned and marched off. Spike then said something to George, who shrugged it off and peace descended on the poolside.

Joe took another drag on his cigarette and sipped more tea. "Something is definitely going on between that crew from Burnley, and I'd love to know what."

Chapter Five

Half an hour later, the two women decided that they needed some sleep.

"By the poolside," Brenda insisted.

"You're sleeping outdoors?" Joe's eyebrows rose.

Sheila clucked. "This is Tenerife, not Scarborough. Of course we'll sleep by the pool."

Seeing them settled on the loungers recently vacated by George and Owen, Joe made his way through reception and out onto the street.

The avenue was split by a central reserve lined with trees. Looking to his right, beyond the nearby hotels and apartment complexes, he could see the motorway and beyond it the hills. Looking the other way, south into the glare of the afternoon sun, he spotted an information board, spelling out the date and time and registering a temperature of twenty seven degrees.

Across the road, he caught sight of George and Owen going into The Mother's Ruin, and it sparked memories of the two months he had been resident here, on the run from Palmanova.

He looked right, road clear, and stepped off the sidewalk. The blare of a car horn brought him up sharp and he looked to the left where a car rushed towards him. He stepped back onto the sidewalk.

He received a torrent of ill-tempered, indecipherable Spanish from the driver, and responded in kind, but in English. "And the same to you." Setting out across the road, he smacked the back of his left hand and cursed himself. "They drive on the wrong side of the road here, you idiot."

Negotiating the crossing, Joe found the interior of The

Mother's Ruin pleasantly cool after the searing heat of the pavements.

After fleeing Palmanova making his way to Tenerife via a roundabout route, the need to keep his location secret meant he could not access his bank or credit cards, and he was faced with having to earn money, which in turn compelled him to take a job at the pub as a short order cook. Working evenings, he had been rushed off his feet. The place was packed seven nights a week, mainly with British tourists, many of them regulars who knew of the pub's fine ales, good if simple food, and quality entertainment.

But now, it was empty. Most Brits, he reasoned, would be enjoying the universal sunshine for which the island was renowned. George and Owen sat in one corner, intent upon a large screen TV hung on the opposite wall, which showed Sky Sports News following the afternoon's English football. Behind the bar, a large, powerfully-built man stood reading a newspaper, while alongside him, polishing glasses, stood a portly, dark-haired waif.

Neither of them appeared to have noticed him. He ran his eyes along a line of beer pumps, the labels so familiar to him. "Give us a pint of bitter and look sharp about it."

It was a prompt for the barman to look up. "What?"

Joe grinned. "Sorry, pal. I was expecting Paddy McLintock." He enhanced the lie. "You look a bit like him."

"He sold up last year." The accent was London as near as Joe could place it. "On his way back to Blighty last I heard."

Joe offered his hand. "Joe Murray. West Yorkshire."

"Ken Lowfield. Slough in years gone by. And this is my wife, Mariella."

Joe shook hands and acknowledged the woman with a polite nod.

Lowfield asked, "So what did you want?"

"Best bitter, one pint of."

Lowfield placed the glass back under the bitter pump. "You were married to Alison, right?"

"She's obviously told you about me."

"Her and Paddy. You worked here in the kitchen for a

while, so legend has it. You looking for work now? Only I could do with a decent short order cook."

"Not likely. I'm on holiday and I'm only here for the week." He cast a nod to the corner where George and Owen were concentrating on the television. "I see you've met a couple of my people. Sanford 3rd agers."

George gave him a cheery greeting. "Hey up, Joe. Terrible twosome had enough of you, have they?"

"They took your loungers at the pool and they're sleeping the flight off. What about you two? Not like you to follow football news."

"Maybe I'll win the pools," Owen said, "and then I won't have to go home next Saturday."

Joe smiled. "Nothing like wishing your life away."

George took a mouthful of beer and pouted in admiration. "Not a bad brew considering how far we've come for it."

"If you don't like it here, you can always bugger off down to Scotch Corner," Lowfield invited.

George grunted. "Shurrup whinging, man." To Joe he said, "It's just like calling in at The Lazy Luncheonette for breakfast. Every order comes free with moans, groans and insults."

"Yeah, well, you shouldn't be so awkward." Joe carried on grumbling to Lowfield. "Bloody customers. Never know what they want and when they don't get it, they do nothing but whine."

Lowfield agreed with him. "There goes the voice of experience."

"I put up with these guys six days a week."

"I picked up their accent and figured here's another coupla moaning northerners." Lowfield placed the glass on the bar. "There you go. Three euros."

Joe took out his wallet. "And get yourself and your good lady one."

"Okey-dokey. Call it five for cash."

Joe handed over the money, and sipped the head from his beer. "Oh, God. Just think you have to travel all this way for a decent pint." He put the glass on the bar. "So how's life in

Las Américas?"

"Same as, mate, same as." He put his newspaper to one side. "Mind the store for a few minutes, Mariella." To Joe, he suggested, "Come on, let's get a cough and spit."

"Catch you in a minute, Ken." Joe joined his fellow members, took out his tobacco tin and began to roll a cigarette. "While I'm putting this together, George, tell me what happened at the swimming pool earlier."

George frowned, his broad features creasing, highlighting the sweat under his brow. "Me and Owen got an hour's kip and sussed out a bit of eye candy."

Joe tutted. "Eye candy. You've been surfing the web again, haven't you? When did you stop calling women, 'talent'? And that's not what I'm talking about, you clown. What happened with those two kids and the older guy? The Wade couple and Harry Givens."

"Oh, that. The two kids had just settled down and the older bloke started giving 'em some earache. The young lad, threatened the older bloke with a good pasting, the older one said summat like, 'by the time you're big enough you'll be too old,' and the kid was about to get up and go for it, when I got sick of hearing it, so I told 'em both to knock it off. The old guy then warned the kid that he'd see him later, and when he cleared off, the kid told me to mind my own business." George grinned. "What's up, Joe? Looking for summat to poke your nose into while you're here?"

Joe licked the cigarette paper and completed rolling the narrow smoke. "You know what I'm like, George. I've been bumping into Givens and the Wades all day. And I don't believe in coincidences."

"They're from Lancashire, Joe. What would you expect?"

"Civilised behaviour." Joe picked up his glass, got to his feet. "I'll be outside with the landlord. Catch you later."

The Mother's Ruin was fronted by a small, outdoor terrace, its canopy keeping at bay the searing heat of the tropical sunshine. Settling down with Lowfield just outside the door, dragging an ashtray to him and lighting up, Joe luxuriated in the fresh, warm air and a light, cooling breeze.

Watching the comings and goings of local people and holidaymakers on the broad avenue, he recalled a club outing to Filey, some years previously. That had seen them enjoy a searing heat wave, but there was none of the relaxed feeling that had enveloped him since his arrival in Torviscas.

"It's almost like I've left all the hassles back home."

Lowfield's broad face had the deeper tan that went with long exposure to stronger sun than the British variety. His thin hair was greying slightly at the temples, but the blue eyes burned with a humour totally at odds with his general demeanour.

He lit a cheroot. "Word is you left in a bit of a hurry last time. Did you get that business sorted out?"

Joe let out a cloud of cigarette smoke with a satisfied hiss. "The woman's locked away for a good many years. Mental hospital, I think. She was certainly a few coppers short of the full shilling. With her locked up, and me back in Sanford, I went back to running my place. It's what I'm best at."

"I know Sanford," Lowfield said. "I used to be a sales rep for a bar fitting company, and I did quite a few pubs in your area."

"You probably know my place, then, but it would have been Joe's Café in those days." Joe dragged on his cigarette. "So, how long have you been out here?"

"About fifteen years. Came for a holiday, liked it so much I got a job in a bar, and aside from the odd week off, I've never been home." Puffing on his cheroot, Lowfield set it on the ashtray, leaned back, stretched and yawned. Despite the length of time he had been resident on the island, he had lost none of his West of London drawl. "Pace of life is different out here, mate. I meanersay, as a cook, you probably never started work until five in the afternoon, and the rest of the time, you just lazed around doing nothing. I have the same business worries as you have back home, but the sunshine scares the tax people and the repo men away." His face became slightly more serious. "Your ex was a bit gloomy, doomy when you went back, you know. Listening to her, I think she was hoping you might hang on here."

Joe sighed. "We discussed it, and don't think I didn't seriously consider it, but Playa de Las Américas needs another Brit café like I need another dozen visits from the VAT man. Besides, if I lived here, I wouldn't appreciate all this." He threw out an open hand, a gesture of approval at the glorious weather.

Lowfield leaned back again, and gave Joe a broader view of the street, and a middle-aged woman walking towards them. She was dressed in white shorts and a navy blue top. He couldn't see her eyes through large, white-framed sunglasses, but there was something about her dark hair that called to Joe.

He dismissed it as a mild fantasy and concentrated on Lowfield once more. "I've been here less than four hours and I can see where you're coming from. It must have taken a lotta bottle to say, 'sod it, I'm not going back'."

"Not really. Divorced, and I had no ties back then. I have now. Mariella." Lowfield nodded towards the bar.

Joe laughed. "In each other's pocket twenty-four-seven? That's what split me and Ali up in the first place."

He concentrated on the woman coming towards them. There was definitely something familiar about the swing of those broad hips and sensuous movement of the heavy breasts. Who was she?

"This is the island of eternal spring, me old china," Lowfield was saying, "and you know what they say about a young man's fancy in the spring."

Joe was not listening. He was intent on this woman. If it were not for the tan, she could well be…

She stopped behind Lowfield. Stared at Joe for a long moment, and then smiled. And in that moment Joe wondered why he hadn't registered her as she approached.

"Hello, Joe. Good to see you again, but what brings you back?"

"Initially, an Airbus 320."

Lowfield whipped his head round, looked at her, then back at Joe, then back at her. "Hello, Ali."

"Hiya, Ken."

Joe was annoyed with himself. It wasn't that long ago when he was here, working with her, sleeping in the spare bed of her apartment. Why didn't he recognise her when she was walking towards the bar?

Lowfield excused himself, returned to the bar, and Ali took his place. "We've been expecting you, and the whisper was you were due in today."

Joe chuckled. "I forgot about the Las Américas grapevine. It's faster here than it is in Sanford, and that's saying something."

Ali excused herself, disappeared into the bar, and returned a few minutes later with a glass of red wine.

"Tell Ken to add it to my bill," Joe instructed.

"So what is it, Joe? Just a holiday? Or have you come back to see me?"

"Let's not fool each other, Ali." He smiled amiably. "Sheila had a bad time of things before Christmas, so we're here with the 3rd Age Club. Convalescence."

Ali demanded all the gory details, and over the next twenty minutes, he told her Sheila's problems in the run-up to the previous Christmas.

"Poor sow."

Joe recalled that Ali regularly read the Sanford Gazette online. "I'm surprised you don't know about it. The Gazette was full of it."

"I probably did. But you tend to forget such trivia here. You know what it's like, Joe. You were here for long enough."

He took out his tobacco tin and began to roll a second cigarette. "Has the local Brit rag been letting everyone know that I was on my way back here?"

Sipping her wine, playing with the glass, Ali nodded. "I told you last time you were here that the Brit community in this place is small and close-knit. A bit like Sanford, only warmer, with more visitors, better views and more pleasant company. News that the great Joe Murray was on his way back, along with members of the Sanford 3rd Age Club, has been kicking round the bars for the last month or more. I'm surprised they didn't put out a tickertape welcome for you when you checked into the Atoll."

Joe suddenly understood the conversation with Pablo on his arrival at the hotel. He jerked a thumb back at the bar. "I was surprised that Paddy had sold up."

"A bit more to it than that, and Ken is like you. Surly, mean, miserable when he likes. He's only interested in his investments and the sports pages, and he doesn't do gossip. Paddy had problems back home." Ali shuffled in her seat and drank more wine. "Anyway, when I learned that you were due in across the road, I thought I'd stroll down and see you. And you know what this place is like." She jerked a thumb at the bar. "I won't have five minutes to myself tonight, and I didn't want you pestering while I'm behind the bar."

"So your announcement when you first saw me was just an ice-breaker?"

"I specifically asked what brought you to The Mother's Ruin," Ali reminded him, "not what brought you to Tenerife. I was gonna go over to the Atoll." She pointed further down the road and the crossing Joe himself had used to get to the pub. "I know everyone round here, including Nina, Pablo and their pals on reception there. They'd have let me through. Either that or they'd have taken a message for you. Then I saw you here."

Joe held his arms out, inviting her to look him over. "Well now that you've seen me, how do I look?"

"Scrawny, underfed. Is Brenda Jump draining your energy, or Sheila Riley emptying your wallet after what happened to her?"

He knew Ali was having a gentle dig at him, but the comment annoyed him all the same.

"They came on board to help after you walked out," he reminded her. "And we're friends. Nothing more. We were all friends, weren't we? Right from our school days. Well, for once, she needed my help."

"Sorry, Joe. You're right, that was uncalled for."

A difficult silence hung between them. Joe looked past her and across the road to the Atoll, where Harry Givens had just emerged from the supermarket and was unwrapping a pack of cigarettes as he ambled along.

Feeling his gorge rising, Joe looked past her again, following Givens as he made his way along the parade of restaurants beneath the Atoll. He paused at one or two, speaking to the greeters. Further along he came to Laurel's English Restaurant and stopped. Once more he spoke to the greeter, then stepped inside, avoiding the outdoor tables. There was no front to block Joe's view and he could see clearly Givens shaking hands with a large, jovial man, Manuel Ibarra, whom Joe knew to be the proprietor.

He brought his focus back to Ali, "I didn't trail two thousand miles to pick a fight with you… or to pick up from where we left off last time I was here."

"No." Alison's tones were more amenable, "and I came out early to find you, not dredge up ten-year-old arguments."

Joe was looking past her again. It seemed to him that Givens had just handed something to the proprietor of Laurel's – and it looked like money.

"What are you looking at?" Ali turned her head as she asked the question.

"See him coming out of Laurel's? I've been bumping into him since we were on the plane."

Ali studied him a moment, then faced Joe. "Harry Givens?"

Joe's eyebrows rose. "You know him?"

"Everyone round here knows him, Joe." She raised both arms and gestured at the street. "Detective Inspector Harry Givens of the Lancashire Constabulary."

Lifting his glass to take another draught of ale, Joe stopped and plonked the glass back down on the table. "He's a cop?"

Finishing her glass of wine, Ali nodded slowly. "He comes out here about four times a year, always stays at the Atoll. We all know him."

"All right, so why is he handing money to Manny?"

"He's a good loser." Ali chuckled. "He should be. He gets plenty of practice playing poker with Ken and Manny over at

Laurels." She jerked her head sideways at the pub to indicate her boss, then at the restaurant, where Givens had concluded his business, gave the proprietor a cheery wave and walked on.

Joe tried to hide his surprise. "I don't remember Paddy playing poker when I was here last."

"Paddy didn't, but Ken does. They usually play after lock up. From two in the morning."

He could not hide his surprise this time. "When does Ken sleep?"

"Not very often." Ali laughed again as she got to her feet. "It's nice seeing you again, Joe. Maybe we should have a meal together, or something."

Still thinking about Harry Givens, Joe took the hint. "Is Monday still your night off?" He waited for her to nod. "Well how about we meet here on Monday evening? Seven o'clock?"

Ali agreed. "You paying?"

"Yes, yes, I'll pay."

She smiled again and kissed him on the cheek. "I'll see you then if not before. And don't be late."

Chapter Six

By mutual consent the members of the Sanford 3rd Age Club decided that Sunday would be a day of rest, a day when they were left to her own devices, to recuperate from the largely sleepless Saturday and the long journey to this idyllic holiday hotspot.

For Joe, it made little difference. He was still up, out of bed a little after half past six, thirty minutes before sunrise. He showered, shaved, made a cup of tea, and then sat out on his balcony, enjoying his first cigarette of the day watching the growing dawn.

He and his friends spent Saturday evening in The Mother's Ruin where a Tom Jones lookalike entertained the packed bar for over an hour. But Joe, Sheila and Brenda were too tired to appreciate the young man's efforts, and they returned to their hotel a little after eleven o'clock. Joe bade the women 'good night' at their door, returned to his apartment, drank a final cup of tea, smoked a final cigarette, and then went to bed, slightly before midnight.

He slept through the night; a consequence of near exhaustion in his opinion, but here he was, six and a half hours later, up and about. That was a consequence of a life spent crawling out of bed in the early hours of the morning.

Even so, a feeling of unaccustomed peace had come over him ever since they arrived, ever since he first looked out on the placid view from his balcony. Back home, the moment he crawled out of bed, his mind slipped into gear, anticipating the day ahead, reminding him of stocks which may be needed, deliveries which were scheduled, preparing him for the highs, lows, ups, downs of running a small business in a busy town in the heart of industrial West Yorkshire. Here he had no such worries. They were Lee's concern for the coming week, not his. Short of his nephew setting fire to The Lazy Luncheonette (something which had actually happened during an Easter weekend in Blackpool) Joe could wallow in the subtropical indulgence surrounding him.

There was nothing on the schedule for the day. Sheila and Brenda, he knew, would indulge in a little retail therapy after breakfast, and he would join them. For all his complaints about their shopping habits, he secretly enjoyed wandering the small souvenir shops, seeking out those quirky, individual items which would remind him of this week in the years to come. But he had no intention of spending the entire day trailing round the shopping areas of Playa de Las Américas. He was on downtime, and meant to make the most of it, doing as little as possible.

Inevitably there were niggles: Harry Givens handing over money to Manny, the proprietor of Laurels, the revelation that Givens was, in fact, a police officer, the readily apparent antipathy between the Wades and Givens, which, considering they all came from the same area of Lancashire, probably had its roots back home.

As Ali had suggested, the business with Givens was quite innocent. Joe was familiar with many police officers, and he was aware that a good number of them were drinkers and gamblers. It was a means of releasing the stress associated with their work, and there was nothing seriously suspicious about it. Owen Frickley was a gambler, and often boasted that year-on-year, he came out ahead of the bookie and casino.

Joe reasoned that these nagging questions were symptomatic of his naturally suspicious and inquiring mind, and his interest in the obvious enmity between Givens and the Wades was another symptom of that most prevalent of human behaviour: nosiness, the natural inclination of people wanting to know what was going on in order to provide a topic for gossip.

Over and above all this, he had the pleasure of Ali's company to look forward to on Monday evening. He had said nothing to Sheila and Brenda. He believed that Sheila was probably still too sensitive to such subjects, and with gossip in mind, Brenda would not hesitate to spread the word. Indeed, by the time she had set the Chinese whispers did the rounds, he and Ali would be getting ready to call the banns for the second time.

He passed the next couple of hours on his balcony, making cup of tea after cup of tea, enjoying his cigarettes, his laptop open on the table in front of him, and he made occasional notes as he observed the locals going about their business, and holidaymakers in the hotel complex opposite and behind The Mother's Ruin, laying out the towels on sun loungers. Without leaning over the balcony to check, he knew that the same routines would be in progress around the Atoll's pool, by the time he, Sheila and Brenda got down there, loungers, space in general, would be at a premium.

And yet, he felt no anxiety, no rush to get down there and bag three sunbeds for their use. He was quite content to take in the sunlight sparkling on the Atlantic, follow the track of the hydrofoil making its way to and from La Gomera, listen to the chime of church bells calling the faithful to Sunday prayers and watch the predictable antics of the sun worshippers at the rear of the surrounding hotels.

Peace, perfect peace, disturbed at half past nine by the buzz of his doorbell. Before he opened the door, he knew it was Sheila and Brenda. Both suitably attired in shorts and tops, Brenda's rather skimpier than Sheila's, both eager for breakfast and the inevitable shopping.

Wearing only a pair of plain blue shorts, and a white T-shirt, Joe put on his gilet, loaded the pockets with everything he would need, and completed his attire with a money belt, in which he kept his passport, wallet, and currency. Tucking it under his shirt, ensuring that the balcony door was locked, he stepped out of the apartment, and joined his two colleagues for a slow, lazy day wandering around the San Eugenio area.

***

The Mother's Ruin was packed both inside and out. On the dais a Neil Diamond tribute act poured out songs from the 1970s, to the delight of the audience. A small area in front of the tiny stage had been cleared, and a few people, amongst them Brenda and George Robson, were dancing to tunes they had grown up with.

Sheila and Joe sat it out, with their backs to the open portals which let in some of the cool, night air. Two members of the bar staff, one of them Ali, made the rounds of the interior and exterior tables, collecting glasses, and taking occasional orders from customers who were either too drunk or too lazy to go to the bar.

When he stopped to think about it, Joe realised he was enjoying himself. Not something he could often lay claim to. The music was good, the beer was better, and the company suited him. It was a good night.

And it came on the back of what had been a good day.

At the lower end of *Avenida de España* was a small c*entro comercial*, a compact shopping centre where they found an acceptable English breakfast, and plenty of shops Sheila and Brenda could browse and pick up occasional items, while Joe sat the session out, taking occasional refills of his coffee. When the women returned, they enjoyed a final drink, before making their way back to the Atoll.

By then it was twelve noon and some of the people less inclined to laze the day away had vacated sun loungers, and Joe commandeered three at the edge of the pool. They spent the entire afternoon there, alternately sleeping, reading, topping up with occasional drinks and food from the pool bar, and at six o'clock, with the sun dipping towards the Western horizon, they made their way back to their respective apartments to get ready for the evening. By eight o'clock, they were in Laurel's, Joe enjoying a traditional, British roast beef and Yorkshire pudding, Brenda and Sheila choosing more continental meals, and finally at nine o'clock, they made their way across the road to The Mother's Ruin.

If anyone noticed how much Joe was drinking, no one commented upon it. Sheila, as always, sipped her gin and tonics in moderation, Brenda indulged her taste for Campari and soda, and Joe sank pint after pint, quenching his thirst, determined to let loose the reins of his usual reserve, but equally determined not to get drunk.

He would fail. By eleven o'clock, when the entertainer was bringing his act to an end, he was rolling in his seat.

Ali had been too busy to spare any time for him, but a couple of times as she passed, she reminded him of the arrangement for Monday evening. She was circumspect. She spoke only when Sheila and Brenda were away from the table, and even then it seemed to Joe that she was slightly beset with other matters, but he guessed it was the pressure of work, and it never occurred to him that her concern was for his potential inebriation.

With the time coming up to half past eleven, Sheila and Brenda were becoming quite vocal on the need to leave before the karaoke session, which would go on until one in the morning, Joe was struggling to finish off his final beer, having chased the previous one down with a couple of whiskies.

And into the general area of festivity walked Spike Wade. The thunderous look on his face told its own tale, and he spent several minutes looking around the bar before lighting on Harry Givens. Tabby gripped his arm as if to restrain him, but he shrugged her off, strode through the crowded tables, and towered over Givens. There followed a lot of finger-pointing, arm waving – some of it in the direction of Tabby – from both men, before Spike reached for Givens' shirt.

At that point, Ken Lowfield marched from behind the bar, laid a hand on Spike's shoulder and turned him away from Givens. It looked like an automatic reaction, but Spike lashed out at Lowfield who ducked back to avoid the flying fist. His face a mask of fury, Lowfield threw a punch, which struck Spike alongside his nose, and sank him to the floor.

The bar was suddenly in pandemonium, with people crying out. Lowfield ignored them all, yanked Spike to his feet, dragged him to the exit, and threw him out onto the pavement. He exchanged sharp words with Tabby, who hurried from the bar to attend to her husband.

Sheila watched the couple walk away in the general direction of the Atoll Spike clutching at his nose. Brenda, meanwhile, crossed the floor and bent before Harry Givens' table to pick up a smartphone. She spoke briefly to Givens who shook his head.

She returned to the table and held up the phone. "We think it belongs to Spike Wade. We have to get it back to him."

"An utter dis... disgrace." Joe's words were slurred. "Give... give it me, and I'll take it back to him in the morn... morning."

Brenda appeared reluctant, but Sheila agreed with Joe. "He's better at that kind of thing, Brenda. Well, he is when he sobers up."

Brenda handed the phone over. "As long as he remembers."

Joe scowled. "When... when did I ever for... forget anything?"

"You want me to write a list?"

Chapter Seven

The warble of his smartphone, playing the main theme to a popular sci-fi movie, woke Joe.

He reached to the bedside cabinet, picked up the instrument, and swept a shaking finger down the lock screen. The menu window read 'Ali', and above it, he scarcely registered the time at ten a.m.

In a life of early mornings, an average Monday would see him out of bed just after half past four. The fatigue of Saturday, the exceptionally early start, the four and a half hour flight, nothing more than a half-hour nap during the late afternoon, and two nights of serious, heavy drinking at The Mother's Ruin, had obviously taken their toll upon him.

His tongue was furred, his head pounded insistently, and he could hardly trust himself to speak as he swept the same wobbly finger across the screen to make the connection.

"Ali?" His voice was not much better than a croak. "What the hell are you doing ringing at this time of day? And on your day off?"

"Just checking you were all right after last night. You were well tanked up, Joe."

"Not the first time you've seen me like that. What are you worrying about?"

"I'm not worried. I'm just making sure you'll be all right to treat me to dinner tonight. You promised. Remember?"

He had forgotten about it. He cleared his gagging throat. "Oh. Yeah. I hadn't forgotten. Listen, I'm still in bed. I'll catch up with you later."

"You'd better."

With the feeling that there was something he had to do, he crawled out of bed, staggered to the bathroom, and ran the shower. A quarter of an hour later, dressed in a pair of gaudy, orange and white shorts and a T-shirt, he made his first cup of tea of the day, stepped out onto the balcony, and sat down, taking in the view across the near Atlantic to La Gomera.

The scene was as calming as he had come to anticipate, and it improved after an infusion of paracetamol to calm his hangover. There was a time in his life when this condition was part and parcel of Sunday mornings, but that was many years in the past and this was Monday. These days he drank in moderation, usually half pints, and not too many of those. Last night, he must have downed six or seven full pints, and although he could not remember, he was sure he finished the night off with a couple of small whiskies. Right now, he needed something to eat, line his stomach, and years of cooking breakfast for others put him off the idea of cooking his own in the apartment. Better to wait for Sheila and Brenda to appear on their balcony, and he would treat them to breakfast at one of the many cafés fronting the Atoll.

They were ahead of him. As he finished his cup of tea, washed up the cup and saucer, and put on his ubiquitous gilet (he always claimed he needed the pocket space) his doorbell buzzed and he opened it to find the two women waiting for him.

"Sobered up?" Brenda's face was split into a broad grin.

She was appropriately dressed for the Canary Islands, wearing only a pair of flip-flops on her feet, and a single piece, floral patterned top and shorts. In Joe's opinion, she was showing too much skin, but he put that down to his delicate condition.

Sheila was similarly dressed, but her attire was darker in colour, and her tan from the Cape Verde Islands had not quite faded, leaving her looking less like a newly arrived holidaymaker. Both women sported expensive sunglasses, reminding Joe that he needed to protect his eyes.

Getting out of bed was not the only lead they had over him. They had already been out, walked along the hotel front seeking a suitable eatery, and eventually decided on the Atoll's pool bar.

"They do a good, cheap full English. Cheaper than that place yesterday." Brenda led the way towards the far end of the peanut-shaped swimming pool. "And you can add it to your bill if you like."

"What bill? This was a package deal, remember. We paid for everything in advance."

"Yes, Joe, but we're here on a self-catering basis." Sheila led the way over the little bridge which crossed the pool to the shaded area of the bar. "All Brenda's saying is that you don't have to pay for it now if you don't want. You can add it to your bill, and settle up before we leave next Saturday."

"Let's keep the books balanced, eh?"

A quarter of an hour later, they were tucking into that same full English breakfast, Joe reserving his criticism for the 'rubbery' egg and stringy bacon, while praising the coffee. He was not a big coffee drinker, but he had always insisted he could only drink the stuff in southern Europe.

"Remember that place in Amsterdam? The coffee was like nitric acid. Played hell with my stomach."

During the meal, Sheila and Brenda brought him up to date with their adventures that morning.

"We booked the Teide tour for tomorrow and the round the island tour for Thursday, and you owe us a hundred euros."

Joe took out his wallet. "When is this again?"

"The first is tomorrow. Coach leaves the front of the hotel at ten o'clock. It gets us back here for about half past four."

Brenda smacked her lips in anticipation. "Apparently, it calls back via a perfume factory somewhere on the West Coast."

Joe recalled Givens mentioning it when they were queueing for the aircraft's toilets. "Guido Isadora, somewhere. I did tell you on the plane"

Sheila tutted. "Guia de Isora."

"For all I know about it, it might as well be Guido Isadora. What are you doing for the rest of today?"

"As little as possible. Just like yesterday." Brenda eyed the sun loungers. "A little more work on my tan, maybe take an hour off for a bit of retail therapy, and then get some rest before filling the alcohol tank again tonight."

Joe clucked irritably. "Canary Islands. The way you carry on, it might just as well be Cleethorpes. You don't do anything different."

Brenda looked down her nose at him. "Yes, but there's a difference between a Tenerife tan and a Cleethorpes cold."

Sheila finished her breakfast, set the plate to one side, and dabbed her lips with a napkin. "Oh, Joe, did you take young Mr Wade's phone back."

Joe silently cursed himself. "I knew there was something I was supposed to do. I'd forgotten all about it." He gulped down the rest of his coffee. "Tell you what, why don't you two grab some sun loungers, I'll nip back to the apartment, get his jelly bone, take it to him and join you in about half an hour."

Brenda's eyebrows rose. "Half an hour? What are you gonna do? Jump into bed with his missus?"

Joe delivered an insouciant grin. "If I can find some way of getting rid of her better half, I might just." He laughed at their disapproving frowns. "No, I'm gonna nip out and pick up some cheap, Tenerife smoke. Half an hour."

For a man of his age, Joe had always been fairly fit. His job was demanding, and he was on the go most of the day when he was behind the counter of The Lazy Luncheonette, and the heat of the kitchen was compatible with the daytime temperatures here in the Canaries. However by the time he got back to apartment 401C, he found his energy almost drained. Automatically, he put the blame on the previous night's alcohol.

He collected the phone, made his way along the landing. As he did so a vague memory called to him. The previous night he had accidentally swept drunken fingers over the lock screen, and equally accidentally opened up Wade's text messages. He was sure it had puzzled him.

Unable to contain his curiosity, he did the same again and learned he remembered right. The message was a puzzle. It was an outgoing message to a number not recognised by the phone, and it read, *apatedolos on*.

Joe assumed it was some kind of code. But to whom? Concerning what?

He would have asked, but he remembered the advice of his two friends. Whatever secrets the Wade's kept from each other or the world at large, were no concern of anyone but themselves. He closed the screen and locked the phone again. Wade's fault, he reasoned. He should have locked his phone with a password.

He rang the bell of the Wades' apartment.

Spike opened the door, looking considerably worse for wear and sporting a prominent black eye.

"That's the problem with being in the wars, lad?"

Spike returned a weak smile. "Tell you what, that landlord packs a hell of a wallop. "

Joe held up the phone. "He does. And your little tête-a-tête is the very reason I'm returning this. One of my girls found it on the pub floor after Ken threw you out."

"Ah. I wondered where it had got to."

From inside the apartment, Tabby called out, asking who was there, and Spike responded accordingly.

He took the phone from Joe. "Come in a minute, Joe. I need a quick word."

Joe followed him in, and nodded a greeting to Tabby, who responded with a curt, silent nod as she made her way out onto the balcony.

Passing the bedroom, Joe noticed that of the twin beds, one of them was neatly made up, but the other was dishevelled, obviously having been slept in. As they entered the living area, he also noticed that the bed settee was covered in sheets and blankets, and a pillow propped at one end.

Spike gave an embarrassed little laugh. "I'm not Tabby's favourite person this morning."

Joe accepted the explanation, even though his mind automatically queried it. The bedroom, like his, did not enjoy a double bed, but twins, so why would his wife compel him to sleep on the settee?

"You wanted a word?"

Spike reached into the fridge, took out a carton of orange juice and poured himself a glass. He offered the carton to Joe, who refused.

"You seemed pretty chummy with Lowfield."

Joe opted to remain non-committal. "I wouldn't say chummy. I spent a couple of months here a little while back, and I worked for the guy who owned the bar before him. Casual. You know. Short order cook."

"Is the place always that violent?"

Once again, Joe chose to remain strictly neutral. "It wasn't when Paddy McLintock ran the place. There was the odd rumble, yes, but I wouldn't say violent. Let's face it, Spike, Brits can be some of the lousiest visitors to any foreign resort, and while he's waiting for the cops to turn out, his bar could be wrecked. If you don't mind me asking, what was the argument about?"

"Something and nothing. That guy, him from Burnley, was giving Tabby the glad eye. I'd had a few beers by then, and I stepped out of line a bit. It shouldn't have happened, but it seemed to me that Lowfield was all on Givens' side."

"Couldn't tell you. I don't remember Ken Lowfield or Harry Givens from the last time I was here. In fact, I only met Harry on the plane. I noticed you had some aggro with him when you got here on Saturday. Was it the same issue?"

"Exactly the same. I mean, what makes him think a girl like Tabby would be interested in a crumbling old git like him?"

Joe laughed. "Some of us crumbling old gits have a lot of mileage left in us, but I know what you mean. Listen, Spike, I'm not one for preaching, but take it from me, fighting never gets you anywhere. I'm too short to get into a rumble and every time I do, I come off worst. Best thing you can do is avoid Givens. It'll only spoil your holiday."

"Yeah. Message understood." Spike fingered his injured eye. "After last night, I think you might be right."

Joe came away from their apartment with the feeling that there was a good deal more wrong than Harry Givens fancying Tabby Wade, but as he passed through reception and out into the street, he reasoned that it was probably his naturally suspicious mind hard at work, and in any case, it was still none of his business.

The supermarket attached to the corner of the Atoll went under the name of Marilyn's, and inside, Joe found it like Aladdin's cave. Every conceivable item he could think of was for sale, right down to water wings, inflatable sun loungers, snorkel masks and a range of beach clothing to fit everyone from children to the George Robsons of this world. This was alongside the usual goods found in a supermarket: chilled and frozen foods, bread, cereals, and more expensive, imported items, like cans of corned beef, spam, baked beans with familiar, British labels. Aside from the prices, which were hiked to account for the cost of importing them, it was like walking round a local branch of any British national supermarket.

He was irritated to learn that they did not sell tobacco, except for tailor-made cigarettes, and those were only available from a machine.

"You have to go to tobacco shops," the young girl manning the checkout told him. "They are easy to recognise. It says *Tabac* over the door."

And of course, Joe knew. He'd come across the same situation so often in other Spanish resorts, but he'd had the idea that things were different in the Canaries. Another amnesiac effect of his hangover?

As he came out of the shop empty-handed, he bumped into Harry Givens, who was checking his wallet. Joe could see it contained a large wad of notes.

"Bit risky that, Harry? Not worried about getting mugged?"

The other laughed. "I tend to look after the pennies, Joe, and I never use plastic when I'm abroad. The credit card companies are just as bad as the street muggers." He tucked his wallet into the side pocket of his baggy shorts. "Settled in okay?"

"Nice place. and Ken keeps a nice pint. I worked there, you know. When Paddy owned it."

"Aye, Ken told me, and I think you mentioned it back in Manchester."

Joe's brow creased as he recalled the conversation with Spike and the information Alison had given him. "You know Ken well, do you?"

"I've been coming here for years, Joe. Of course I know him. I knew him when he ran the Maidenhead in Ten Bel, and Kenny's Bar in Las Américas. And he knows me. In fact, we play cards regular. That's why he threw that little snot out last night and only had a quiet word in my ear."

"Funny you should mention that. I've just been speaking to Spike, and he reckons you were eyeing his wife up."

Givens laughed with genuine pleasure. "I'm a single man. I eye up all the women, especially the good looking ones like her. It doesn't mean to say I do anything about it. I mean, my Ma's dog used to chase cars, but he wouldn't know what to do with one if he ever caught it."

The old, variety hall joke did nothing to impress Joe, but he smiled and went on his way, passing through reception, and out to the pool area where he joined his two companions. Brenda went to the bar and came back with three soft drinks, and while they enjoyed the cola, and basked in the increasing heat and glorious sunshine, he told him of the last half-hour.

Sheila tutted her disapproval. "I think it's a shame when people can't go on holiday and learn to keep their tempers. Young Wade would have been better off having a quiet word in Givens' ear. There was no need for fighting."

Brenda expressed the opinion that Givens was an old fool, but accepted Joe's account of his explanation. "In a place like this, there's many a lecherous old sod looking over the female skin from behind their mirror sunglasses."

Joe looked ready to take offence. "Why are you looking at me when you say that?"

"If the cap fits…"

He took a grateful swallow from his glass, and looked Brenda up and down. "You need something more than a cap to cover all that skin."

Brenda pulled her tongue out at him. "Peeping Tom."

Chapter Eight

Joe had sufficient experience of excursions with Sheila and Brenda to know that there was little point complaining about the number of shops they visited – some of them more than once – and the amount of clothing they purchased. A good proportion of it was wholly unsuitable for spring and summer in Tenerife, and the rest completely unsuitable for any time of year in Sanford.

"You'll look absolutely stunning wandering around Sanford market in a low-cut bra and a pair of knickers that wouldn't cover the salt and pepper pots in The Lazy Luncheonette," he told Brenda when she came out of one high-class establishment in Playa de Las Américas.

"It's an itsy-bitsy, teeny-weeny bikini."

"The bits it's supposed to cover aren't so itsy-bitsy or teeny-weeny these days, and if you wore that back home, it's an open invitation to an arrest for indecent exposure."

They dismissed his complaints, ordering him to go looking for his tobacco, and with the benefit of experience, Joe followed their suggestion.

He ambled along the street, and found a supermarket where they sold his tobacco. He purchased five packs, and as he came out, he noticed a camera shop next door.

He was always wary of such establishments. On one visit to the Canaries, he had paid in excess of eighty euros for a compact camera, which, when he returned home, turned out to be worth no more than twenty pounds, had a resolution inferior to his existing compact, and worked with a fixed, two-second delay between pressing the button and taking the picture. Fine for a landscape, but of no use at all if taking pictures of, say, a moving boat or aeroplane.

Consequently, when the proprietor, basking in the sunshine in his doorway, invited him in, Joe shook his head. "Once bitten, twice shy."

"You have been bitten, señor? We have excellent range of insect repellers."

Joe laughed at the mispronunciation of 'repellent'. "I'll bet you do."

He wandered on his way, but as he passed the shop's large display window, he noticed a pair of small binoculars on one of the lower shelves. Not the kind of equipment that would be much use in Sanford. Even through field glasses, buildings were all he would see, or traffic travelling along the distant motorway. But here, he had a wide-open view of the Atlantic, and local boat traffic travelling between Tenerife and La Gomera, aircraft circling on final approach, stars at night (although he could not imagine that such small glasses would show him much more than he could see with his eyes). The price was thirty euros.

It was rare that Joe was impulsive, but for once he buried his inhibitions, and walked into the shop. Twenty minutes later, he came out with the glasses, and a small case to accommodate them, plus a bottle of lens cleaner (which he did not need because he already had a bottle in his luggage along with his Sony camera) and the final bill came to a little short of fifty euros.

Wandering back towards the clothing store where he had left his companions, he made an effort to recall the twenty minutes he had spent with the shopkeeper, trying to pinpoint the man's surreptitious sales skills, and wondering if he could utilise them in The Lazy Luncheonette. He charged about eight pounds for a full English breakfast which included a cup of tea and two slices of toast. If he could slyly add a little marmalade, or one of those appalling hash browns they had served on the plane, he could probably jack the price up to nine pounds, slip the customer his change along with his tea and trust to luck that he wouldn't notice.

Right away, he dismissed the idea. The Sanford Brewery draymen were his most loyal customers, and he made a lot of money from them. They were free and easy, laid-back, but to a man (and woman) they were Yorkshire bred, and counted every penny in change before dropping it in their pockets.

Unwilling to hang about outside fashion shops, he found a small café, selected an empty, shaded table, and ordered coffee. Across the road was an Irish bar, one of the most popular in Las Américas. Next door to it was a genuine, English chippy, run by an English family. During the time he had spent here with Ali, he had visited the place several times, and congratulated the family on capturing the perfect flavour of British fish and chips. Aside from the sunshine and soaring temperatures, he could have been buying them anywhere in Yorkshire.

As he watched, he noticed a young woman and an older man, his arm draped around her shoulder in a manner which suggested he was neither her father nor uncle. The distance was too great for Joe to see clearly, but he was certain it was Harry Givens and Tabby Wade. He scrabbled into the bag containing his new binoculars, retrieved them, feverishly unzipped the case, and took them out, but by the time he put them to his eyes, and adjusted the focus, the couple had gone.

What was it Spike had said about Givens giving Tabby's the eye? What was it Givens said about the way he ogled most young women, but meant nothing by it? He saw Givens handing over money to Manuel Ibarra, the proprietor of Laurels. A poker debt? Or a fee in lieu of an introduction?

His twirling thoughts homed in on the fight between Spike and Givens in The Mother's Ruin. Suppose it had nothing to do with Givens eyeing up Tabby. Suppose it was more concerned with negotiating a profitable price for… services rendered?

That notion swung his attention to Spike's phone and the strange message he had read. What was it? Apartmentos Dolos. No. It wasn't that long or complex. He racked his memory, building a visual image of the phone and the message, until he pinned it down. *Apatedolos on.*

Something going down. Maybe something trivial – like an agreement between client and service provider – maybe something more important. He scolded himself for not having checked the time the message was sent. If that was before the fight, then it could possibly have been to Givens, and maybe Givens agreed in principle, and then changed his mind in The Mother's Ruin. As an explanation, it would make a lot more sense than Spike losing his temper because Givens was giving Tabby the visual once over.

It was obviously in code, Joe wondered to himself whether it was something as simple as an anagram. He took out a notebook and pen, wrote down APATEDOLOS, leaving a good space between each letter, and then began to fiddle to see what kind of sense he might make of it.

Twenty minutes later, he was no further forward, when he realised the time was getting on. He was in the process of gathering together his bits and pieces and sorting out change to settle his bill, when Sheila and Brenda turned up, their hands full of carrier bags bearing the fancy logos and names which were a mystery to Joe, but were no doubt well known across the Canary Islands.

"I told you we'd find him here, didn't I?" Sheila said. "A café facing south where he can take the sun, but with enough shade to cool him down."

Joe had intended crossing the road and sampling the delights of the Irish bar. Instead, he sat down again, signalled the waiter, and ordered a fresh cup of coffee for himself, a soft drink for Sheila, and a Campari and soda for Brenda.

He grumbled about the latter, telling her it was too early in the day for alcohol, but Brenda pooh-poohed his protests. "It's never too early in Las Américas."

"We are all shopped out, Joe. Brenda needs the fortification."

Sheila's best friend agreed. "Besides, I'll get a good rest when we get back to the Atoll, ready for you treating us to a slap up feed tonight."

He shook his head. "No can do. I have a prior engagement."

The two women exchange wide-eyed, semi-amused glances, and as the waiter delivered their drinks, Brenda couldn't resist teasing Joe. "You've got a sly date? Is it anyone we know? Like that fit little travel courier? What's her name? Diana?"

Joe grunted. "As if a girl like that would look twice at a silly old f... fool like me. Now, if you must know, it's Ali. We'll be reminiscing under the stars, chewing on a well-done beefsteak."

Brenda sniffed disdainfully. "As opposed to reminiscing under an umbrella and chewing on a battered cod and ten bob's worth of chips like you did on the night you first met her."

"Who paid ten bob for chips back then? It was at least a pound." He sipped his coffee. "Do I need to remind you for the umpteenth time that Ali put me up when I was on the run from that crazy so-and-so in Palmanova? And she helped get me work at The Mother's Ruin. Without her, I'd have been back in England long before I worked out who the killer was. The least I can do is take her out to dinner."

Brenda looked as if she was ready to go into more teasing, but before she could say anything, Joe cut her off.

"Anyway, never mind me and Ali. You wanna hear what I've just seen."

Sipping on her lemonade, Sheila cocked her head to one side. "Isn't that a contradiction in terms? You've seen something, and we need to hear it. How can we hear something that's visual?"

"Stop splitting hairs. You know what I mean."

Over the next few minutes, he told them exactly who and what he had seen. The women listened, occasionally turning to look across the road at the Irish bar and the chippy, about which Joe waxed so eloquently. When he was through, there were several moments of silence, before Brenda asked, "What are you suggesting, Joe? That there's something going on between them?"

"Brenda has a point," Sheila agreed. "For all you know, Harry Givens might be her uncle."

"Well he must be the black sheep of the family if he is. Last night, Spike was fit to knock him all over Torviscas. He probably would have done if Ken Lowfield hadn't stepped in. Just listen a minute, because there's other stuff you don't know about."

He went on to tell them what he had seen outside Laurels, and Ali's explanation for the money changing hands.

Once more his friends were at a loss to understand his interest. "It all sounds reasonable to me," Sheila said.

Brenda agreed. "And me. What exactly are you getting at, Joe?"

"Well, see, I thought she might be, er, you know…" He struggled to put it into polite words. "Charging for special services." His eyes burned into them, willing them to understand.

As always, they understood only too well, and Sheila scolded him. "Really, Joe, the depths your mind sinks to. She's such a sweet girl, modest, almost shy."

"Oh yes? And how many, er, professional women do you know who walk around with a placard hanging round their neck, saying, 'one hundred euros, negotiable'?"

Brenda was slightly more persuaded than Sheila. "Fair comment. But what makes you think she's on the game?"

"It was the way Givens had his arm around her neck. His hand was a little close to her…" He stared pointedly at Brenda's half-bared bosom. "You know."

Brenda's eyes wandered around the café, obviously considering the image Joe had just thrust into her head. "Hmm. I know they're fairly free and easy here, but I should think public groping is still an offence."

"Not if the woman allows it," Joe retorted. Before they could get into the argument, he went on to tell them of the message he had read on Spike's phone, whereupon Sheila took up his pad had read through his attempted anagram-solving.

Her brow knitted. "You've written, 'pasted oloa'. What's oloa?"

Joe shrugged. "It was the only word I could get out of the remaining letters."

Sheila probably disagreed. "No, you could have 'a pasted

loo'."

"But that doesn't make any more sense than oloa." Joe lit a fresh cigarette. "A pasted loo? What are you gonna paste it with?"

Brenda shuddered. "Please. Don't go there. Some of the public lavatories I've seen—"

Sheila interjected in order to prevent a graphic description side-tracking them. "Are you sure it was Harry Givens and Tabby?" Once again, she looked over her shoulder at the Irish bar, judging the distance. "It's a long way. A good fifty, sixty yards at least. You're absolutely certain it was them?"

He shrugged. "All I can say is, the guy was dressed the same as Harry Givens when I met him this morning, and he was the same build. And the woman was a dead ringer for Tabby Wade."

Brenda took another large slug of her Campari. "What I don't understand, is where all this has come from. You told us – was it on the plane – that they all three came from Burnley. Maybe they know each other. All right, all right, that's no excuse for him try to grab one of her bubbles, but that could have been accidental, or it could have been just the angle and distance you were looking from."

Sheila waded in on Brenda's side. "If you're correct, Joe, how do you account for the fighting in The Mother's Ruin the other night?"

Joe was not about to be beaten into submission. "I've thought about that, haven't I? Suppose Tabby tapped him up him in The Mother's Ruin, and suppose Givens tried to get a reduction of, say, twenty or thirty percent. Tabby would have refused, and Givens could have given her a serious mouthful, and then, Spike goes flying in." He shrugged. "It makes more sense than having a go at Givens because he was giving Tabby the eye."

The two women were not persuaded. Sheila, in particular, was scathing. "Back in the day, Peter could be very forthright with men when they tried to, er, pull me? Is that the right word?"

Brenda chuckled. "It'll do. We know what you mean.

Colin was never the jealous type, and I had plenty of men trying to trap off with me, but as long as they didn't go too far, he didn't worry about it."

"You had men trying to trap off with you while you were married?" Joe's eyes goggled.

"You don't have to sound so surprised."

"It's not that. I was just thinking things haven't changed much, have they?"

"Bog off."

They finished their drinks, and left the café. The raw, searing heat of the afternoon hit them the moment they left the shade, and as they made their way to a taxi rank for the three-mile journey back to the Atoll, sweat was pouring from Joe's brow within a matter of minutes. Even with a sun hat pulled low to shade his eyes, the intense heat was intolerable.

Fifty yards on, they came to Kenny's Bar, a compact place, proudly displaying the union jack above its entrance. Joe walked on, but as he glanced in, he spotted Spike at a table towards the rear. He had a smartphone – the one Sheila had recovered and which Joe returned – to his ear, and from the look on his face, it was a serious conversation.

"Belling his lawyer back in England, I'll bet," Joe commented as they continued on their way. "Maybe she's not tipping up enough of her earnings."

"Then again, he could just have heard that his father's been taken seriously ill." Sheila glared at him. "What is it you tell us about making assumptions without evidence to back them up?"

"But I have evidence."

"As long as the couple you saw going into the Irish bar were Givens and Tabby." Brenda opened the rear door of a taxi on the rank, and climbed in. Sheila followed her. "Come on, Joe, it's time to get your wallet out."

Chapter Nine

Putting on a pair of fawn, casual trousers and slipping his feet into a pair of suede loafers, Joe inspected his appearance in the wardrobe mirror. The ensemble was complete with a white, short-sleeved shirt, and the inevitable gilet, and upon self-inspection, he immediately approved.

Back home, an evening out, even with your ex-wife, would demand a suit, collar and tie (and possibly a lawyer, Brenda had joked) but in this heat, and given the laid-back approach of life on the island, his present, smart yet casual attire was ideal. At a pinch, he could leave the gilet behind, but he needed the pocket space, and not only for necessities like tobacco and wallet, but also his inhaler. Surely Alison would understand why he did not get fully spruced up for a meal.

He rang her just after six o'clock, and confirmed their arrangement to meet outside Laurel's at seven.

"I'll be there, but if you think you taking me for a drink to The Mother's Ruin after Manny's place, you've another think coming. That would be like me taking you for a snack to The Lazy Luncheonette."

Joe frowned into the phone. "Manny's place? Manny who?"

"Manuel Ibarra. You remember him. He owns Laurel's. Big mate of Ken Lowfield's. We ate there now and again when you were shacked up in my spare room."

"Oh. Yes. Of course. Okay. You're the guide and tormentor, Ali. It's wherever you want. I'll see you outside Laurel's at seven."

With the arrangements made, he made himself a cup of tea, stepped out onto the balcony, rolled and lit a cigarette.

The sun was setting slowly into the Atlantic, but would keep its head above water for a little over another hour. Below him, people milled along the street, checking out the shops, cafés, restaurants and bars, or simply ambling, hand in hand, arm in arm, enjoying the glow of the subtropical evening. Up above, the strobe lights of a passenger aeroplane winked in the growing darkness, but it was still light enough for him to make out the livery of a well-known, low-cost, British airline.

The feelings of peace and contentment, which had been with him since they first arrived, enveloped him once more. Two thousand miles away, the old country was going through one of its periodic upheavals, political and social, the subject of many a debate in the dining area of The Lazy Luncheonette, and Joe frequently got drawn into the arguments. Not that he had much interest. He could find plenty of more practical, more important arguments, usually concerning money. And yet, for all that any of it mattered, those discussions, often aggressive, sometimes to the point of near fighting, might as well be on the moon. They had no place on this, the Island of Eternal Spring.

His thoughts turned naturally to Ali. When she was younger, when he had proposed, she was a spectacularly attractive woman, and he was both delighted and surprised when she said, 'yes'. She was two decades older, but she had lost none of her beauty. If anything, age had brought with it a greater attraction, and it was still a surprise to him that she was willing to entertain a wizened old scroat like him. She had lived on this island for over five years, and during the brief time he had spent with her on the run from Palmanova, he learned that she could take her pick of the available men in the Las Américas area. Not that she was flighty, or easy, but she could have settled into a relationship with any number of men during her years here.

Why, then, hadn't she? Why was she happy to have dinner with him? And if he knew Ali, it would be more than dinner. Older she might be, but she was no less passionate.

When he thought about it, theirs was a bizarre situation.

He knew plenty of men and women who were divorced; George Robson and Owen Frickley to name but two. But he could not think of any who were able to turn to their ex-husbands/wives in the same way that he had turned to Ali for help when he ran from Palmanova, and by the same token, he could not think of any man or woman willing to help in the way that Ali had.

At just after seven o'clock, with the rim of the reddened sun skimming just above the Atlantic horizon, he left the balcony, washed up the cup and saucer, rolled another cigarette, and ensuring he was well armed with money and particularly the electronic keycard for his apartment, he stepped out onto the walkway, just as Brenda and Sheila were coming from their room.

Brenda looked him up and down. "What the well-dressed man about town is wearing. Is that the best you could do, Joe?"

What was it he had thought about leaving arguments back home? He took immediate umbrage. "What's wrong with it?"

Sheila pursed her lips. "Nothing that a decent pair of trousers, a pair of polished, leather shoes, and a properly pressed shirt wouldn't put right."

"Like hell."

Desperate to find some criticism of their attire, he looked them over, and to his disappointment could find nothing wrong with Sheila's sensible skirt and blouse, or Brenda's pants and loose-fitting top.

"Anyway. It's only a meal with Ali."

Brenda was about to comment, when a piercing cry carried along the deck access.

"What are you gonna do about it?"

It was a female, screaming at the top of her voice. Joe would never have recognised the woman concerned, but he certainly recognised the accent.

It was followed a couple of seconds later by a male, shouting loud enough to be heard all over the Atoll. "Sink you. That's what I'm gonna do."

Joe clucked impatiently. "The Wades. I'd better see what

—"

Sheila interrupted. "Now, Joe, keep out of it."

"Yes, but—"

Brenda took his arm as he turned away. "Sheila's right, Joe. It's an argument between a married couple, and you're old enough to know better than to interfere. At worst, you might get a punch on the nose, but at best, they'll unite, turn on you and tell you to mind your own business before chucking you off the balcony."

As always, when it came to the slightest disagreement between him and the two women, he capitulated. He was never going to win. "Oh well. It's time I was meeting Ali, anyway."

They ambled along towards the lift.

"So where are you two going?"

It was Sheila who answered. "We're going down to the little shopping centre, see what we can't treat ourselves to, then we'll probably get a meal at one of the restaurants across the road, before coming back to The Mother's Ruin. What about you and Alison?"

"Laurel's first, and then a couple of snifters somewhere else, but it won't be The Mother's Ruin. She thinks that would be a busman's holiday."

They parted company in reception, Brenda advising him, "Don't spend too much, Joe."

Sheila confined herself to wishing him a pleasant evening, the two women turned towards the c*entro comercial*, while Joe turned right, and walked up the parade to Laurel's, where Ali was already looking at her watch.

"Late as usual, Joe."

He pecked her on the cheek. "Big argument on our landing. I was gonna put it right, but Sheila and Brenda wouldn't let me."

"I should think not. You don't want blood all over your shirt after someone thumps you. Come on. Manny's got a table for us."

Manuel Ibarra, known to all and sundry as Manny, was a Canary Islander by birth, but a determined anglophile, and spoke perfect English with only the slightest trace of an accent.

Short, tubby, obviously well fed, he confessed to an absolute love of everything English, right down to decorating the walls of his open plan restaurant with a portrait of HM the Queen surrounded by photographs, many of them monochrome, of London's most iconic monuments, including Trafalgar Square, Tower Bridge and Buckingham palace. Spread further around the walls were other, well-known images: a Spitfire, a Lancaster bomber, both reproductions of renowned paintings, the Forth Railway Bridge, Brunel's bridge over the Menai Strait, HMS Ark Royal, further complemented by shots of easily identified seaside towns, and finally publicity stills from some of the UK's best-loved soap operas.

"Home from home," Joe commented as they took an outdoor table.

He had visited the place a couple of times when he stayed with Ali, and he recalled that the tiled ceiling of the interior was broken by regularly spaced, inset lights, each surrounded by highly polished brass borders, which Manny had told him, enhanced the lighting without intruding on the general ambience, and Joe remembered looking up at one of the surrounds and seeing his bizarrely twisted reflection looking back down at him as clearly as if he were in a fairground hall of mirrors.

While they studied the menu, Les Tanner and Sylvia Goodson ambled past on their evening constitutional, and exchanged a few pleasantries before going on their way. Joe frowned after their departing backs, his mind filled with images and content of their gossip at breakfast tomorrow.

He followed them making their way towards the Atoll, and as they reached the entrance, Spike Wade came out. It was difficult to see, but Joe had the impression that he was still annoyed. A hangover from the row he was having with Tabby a quarter of an hour previously? Looking both ways, he hurried across the dual carriageway, and stopped on the central reserve, patting his pockets. With an attitude of absolute frustration, he turned and hurried back to the hotel.

"Must've forgotten his wallet."

"Hmm?"

He focused on Alison. "Sorry. I just saw Spike Wade in a paddy, and turn to go back to the—"

"Joe. Are you having dinner with me or just nosing at everyone else in Torviscas?"

He conceded the point. "You're right. You ready to order?"

Conservative as ever, Joe asked for fruit juice as a starter, and ordered a well done steak for his main course. Ali chose a traditional Spanish prawn cocktail and the same main course as Joe.

Throughout the meal, they kept up a steady, strictly non-controversial chatter, reflecting on life in Sanford and Playa de Las Américas, how their lives had differed since their separation and divorce, and it occurred to Joe that while he was content with his lot, Ali led a much more varied and potentially more exciting life than he.

And he knew that if it were possible, he would be ready to give it another shot, but even as he thought about it, common sense told him that it would never happen. Despite the temptation, he would never leave Sanford and Ali would never return to Great Britain.

A little before nine o'clock, he settled the bill, and they took a taxi down into Playa de Las Américas. Joe left the choice of bar to Ali, and she took him to Kenny's where the evening's entertainment was about to start. It was another tribute act, two women performing as the female half of Abba. Ali had seen the act many times before and Joe was certain he had too.

"If you haven't, they're at The Mother's Ruin later in the week."

"I might just give that night a miss then."

Overall, it was a pleasant evening, and with the time coming up to midnight, they ambled along to a taxi rank, and once in the vehicle, Ali ordered the driver to her apartment on the northern outskirts of the town. Joe sat alongside her in the rear seat, saying nothing. He purposely suppressed any hopes that Ali might invite him in, but when they reached her apartment block, so familiar to him from his time on the run from Palmanova, she insisted that he pay the driver, and come in 'for coffee'.

It was entirely typical of Joe's approach to dealing with women that he left all the running to her. He remembered the nights he had spent sleeping in a camp bed in her spare room, and in particular recalled the one night he had spent in her double bed. That was just before he returned to the UK.

At half past midnight, he was about to leave when Ali stopped him.

"Oh no. You don't get away that easily, Joe Murray."

"Yes, but we're going to see the volcano tomorrow."

"Don't worry. You'll be back at the Atoll in plenty of time to catch your bus… as long as you get out of my bed early enough."

Chapter Ten

Joe's absence was uppermost in the minds of Sheila and Brenda when they arrived for breakfast in the Atoll's restaurant, shortly after half past eight on Tuesday morning, which was where and when they had agreed to meet the other members of the 3rd Age Club while they waited for their bus.

"The dirty stop out," Brenda complained as she settled at the table with a bowl of cereal and a plate of scrambled eggs. "Ali tempted him last night. Offered him a good time back at her place. You know that, don't you?"

Sheila chewed her way delicately through a bowl of muesli. As usual, she was the voice of moderation. "He's over twenty-one, Brenda. He can do as he pleases. So he chose to spend the night with Alison. What of it? I don't think it's going to lead anywhere. If some kind of reconciliation were on the cards, it would have happened when he was here after Palmanova." She gave her best friend a disapproving look. "And you're hardly a model of virtue, are you?"

"I was last night."

Realisation dawned on Sheila. "Ah. You were feeling a little, er, frisky?"

"I was well-oiled." Brenda often found that she could be absolutely candid with Sheila. "And yes, I could have done with some, er, company, and Joe's right next door... Or, he should have been. Wait while I see him, the dirty, sneaky little—"

"Let's just hope he's back in time to catch the bus for Teide."

Although their package included rooms at the Atoll, it did not include meals, but both women noticed that other members of the 3rd Age Club were already in the dining room, all of them scheduled to join the half day trip to the foot of the volcano.

As they worked their way through breakfast, Les Tanner and Sylvia Goodson took the table across the aisle, and Sylvia was as excited as any child ready for the day's excursion.

"It's such a long time since I've been to Teide," she said with that proselytising fervour she reserved for most highlights in her life. "The air up there is so much cleaner and fresher than down here."

Sheila advised caution. "Make sure you have a warm coat with you, Sylvia. Or a cardigan. The air might be fresher up there, but it's also colder."

Tanner, as ever in control of matters, beamed broadly. "Already in hand, my dear." He glanced around and came back to them. "What's happened to our wonderful chairman? Late, or is he crying off?"

"He had a heavy date last night, Les," Brenda reported.

Les chuckled. "Yes, we know. We exchanged a few pleasant words with them as they were ordering dinner outside Laurels. Alison, no less. You don't think there's anything serious in it, do you?"

Sheila's variable mood shifted to disapproval. "No, I don't, but as I've just been saying to Brenda, I don't really think it's any of our business."

Brenda moved her empty cereal bowl out of the way, and tackled her scrambled eggs. "She put him up after that business in Palmanova, and we figured this was Joe's way of saying thank you."

"Oh to be young and still capable of thanking a woman in such a pleasurable manner."

Sylvia sniggered and her response took Sheila and Brenda by surprise, and brought spots of colour to Les's cheeks.

A few minutes later, as they were finishing their coffee, Joe stepped into the dining room, made his way round the self-service area, paid for his meal, and joined them with a gruff, "Morning all."

He tucked into bacon and eggs and ignored their attempts to drag information from him. Alec and Julia Staines arrived, and sat with Les and Sylvia, and once they were brought up to date, they too hassled Joe for the gory details.

Eventually, unable to resist the pressure any longer, he took a swallow of coffee, and declared, "I don't kiss and tell." With a broad grin he asked, "Do I, Brenda?"

She groaned "Thank you very much, Joe Murray. You've just told everyone I'm on your lists of potential conquests."

"I think you fulfilled your potential a long time ago." With another grin, he picked up his knife and fork and returned to his meal. "What time is the bus due?"

"Ten o'clock." Sheila glanced at her watch. "Are you going like that? Because if you want to get changed, you'll have to get a move on."

"Won't take me five minutes... If I can ever finish my breakfast."

From across the aisle Les could not resist further teasing. "So, Joe, is a reconciliation on the cards?"

Joe chewed on a mouthful of rubbery egg, swallowed it, and gave Les's proposition a little mock-thought. "I'm not sure, Les. I don't think you and I can ever be anything but distant friends."

The response brought a gaggle of laughter from the two tables and more disapproval from Les.

Joe washed down the egg with more coffee. "Let's clear the air. There is no prospect of any reconciliation between Alison and me. We get on okay. Better than okay. But she won't go back to Sanford and even though she'd like me to, I won't move to Tenerife."

Alec Staines gaped. "You could move to Tenerife and you won't?"

"That's right, Alec. I find it easier annoying people in Sanford. If I moved here, I'd have to learn to speak proper Spanish first. Now, does anyone mind if I finish my breakfast before we go look at the volcano?"

With the clock reading nine fifteen, Joe disappeared, making his way back to his apartment, and the others filed out of the dining room, into the reception area. Alec Staines and Les Tanner stepped outside for a smoke, and the four women took up the available seating, chatting, reminiscing over previous visits to the Canary Islands. Julia Staines confessed her preference for Fuerteventura, Brenda argued in favour of Tenerife, while Sylvia urged them to try Lanzarote or Gran Canaria. Sheila expressed no preference, but recalled a holiday to Tenerife with her first husband and their children. After her trials and tribulations of the previous year, everyone was careful not to mention the Cape Verde Islands.

While they waited for Joe and the bus, a dishevelled looking George Robson and his pal, Owen Frickley, meandered into the hotel, gave the women a tired wave, and went on their way to their apartment.

"I thought they were supposed to be coming with us," Sylvia commented.

It was Brenda who responded. "They were talking about it, but by the looks of them, they've had a heavy night. We know what they're like."

"Probably elbow bending all night," Julia said.

Brenda sneered. "Or something more horizontal knowing George."

The comment brought a ripple of giggles, but before they could develop the slightly catty conversation any further, Tabby Wade hurried into reception and up to the counter. She was obviously in some distress, and although Pablo kept his voice down, she could be clearly heard.

"My husband. Have you seen him?" Obviously worried that Pablo would not understand her, she translated it into Spanish.

Pablo replied in English. His voice was so muted that they could not hear what he said, but a shrug of his broad shoulders was enough to transmit the message. Tabby rushed out of the hotel, and from their seats, they could see her run into the supermarket next door. She was gone less than a minute, and when she came out, she hurried to the kerb, glanced both ways, then dashed across the road, hurrying into The Mother's Ruin.

She disappeared into the bar, Brenda automatically checked her watch. "Too early for the regular crew. All she'll find are the cleaners."

Julia disagreed. "Ken and his wife live on the premises."

Almost as soon as she said it, Tabby reappeared with Lowfield right behind her, and the two were obviously arguing. Lowfield said something, gesticulated wildly with his arms, Tabby poked him in the chest while she gave him a mouthful by return, and Lowfield grabbed her finger, leaned into her and from the look on his face, he was obviously threatening her. In the end, she turned, and headed back across the road to the Atoll.

Determined to help, Sheila got to her feet, and met her as she rushed into the reception area.

"Tabitha, whatever is the matter?"

Tears streamed down the young woman's face. "Spike. He's missing. I woke up twenty minutes ago, and he wasn't there. They haven't seen him here, and the supermarket manager hasn't, and neither has that ignorant so-and-so across the road."

Sheila took her hand, guided her to a sofa just inside the doors. "I'm sure there's no need to worry. Maybe he's just gone out for a walk."

Tabby shook her head. "He wouldn't do that. Not without telling me first. I've got an awful feeling that something's wrong."

Sheila recalled the argument she, Brenda and Joe had heard the previous evening, but diplomatically did not mention it.

"How long have you been married?"

To her surprise, Tabby seemed uncertain. "Oh... About... About three months. This is supposed to be our honeymoon. We couldn't get time off when we were married, and anyway, who wants to go on holiday the middle of January?"

Sheila patted her hand. "It's a time of adjustment for you both. I mean, I'm assuming you haven't been married before."

"We're not old enough to have that kind of past." The

young woman sniffed back her tears. "We had... Had words last night. One of those silly things. You know. But we were all right when we went to bed." She looked urgently into Sheila's caring eyes. "Something's wrong. He wouldn't go out without telling me where he was going."

Tabby's distress brought memories of Sheila's problems the previous year. For a moment, they threatened to overwhelm her, but she steeled herself, burying the distasteful memories. Her problems were the result of a lack of judgement, while Tabby's could be put down to simple inexperience.

Pulling in a deep breath, letting it out with a sigh, Sheila gently lectured the woman. "I was married for twenty-five years to a wonderful man. He died, you know. Double heart attack. We had many a cross word in our time, and even though Peter would often take himself off after an argument, he was usually back within an hour or two. Marrying, living together, is a whole new way of life, Tabitha. It's different to being on your own, or going steady with a boyfriend, when you have space for yourself. It might be that Spike... What is his proper name?"

"Rodney. Rod. He prefers Spike."

Sheila delivered an encouraging smile, which she feared came out as more of a wince. She had never been in favour of using pet names. "It might be that Spike just needed a little time to himself. Remember, if you're finding marriage strange, he is too. He'll be back soon. You wait and see. And if I know anything about young men and new husbands, he'll probably have a nice bunch of flowers or a box of chocolates for you."

Tabby gazed hopefully into Sheila's concerned face. "You think so?"

"I'm sure of it."

The younger woman sighed. "It's not like him." There was a greater sense of urgency about her. "I can't help getting the feeling—"

Sheila cut her off. "You're a young woman in love. It's natural to be worried. If you'll take my advice, go back to your apartment, make yourself a cup of tea, and try ringing him."

"I already tried. His mobile's turned off. That's another thing. He never switches it off."

Sheila maintained the benign set of her face, but behind it, the first hint of doubt entered her head. It seemed to her that young men and women these days never switched off their mobile phones. Joe often commented that the modern generation would need them surgically removed. A standard, irritable, Joe Murray observation on the world at large, but it was not without foundation. Even here, a holiday paradise, most people, locals and visitors alike, could be seen fooling around with their phones. They could not even enjoy a cup of coffee in an open-air café without tapping or chatting away on them.

Why then would Spike Wade switch his off?

With no obvious answer to the question, she was determined to encourage Tabby. "It sounds as if he really does need a little time to himself. Keep your phone on, Tabitha. He'll be in touch when he begins to miss you."

Chapter Eleven

The seventy-seat bus was barely half full, and most of the passengers were 3rd Age Club members. Their courier was Diana, who greeted them enthusiastically as she ticked them off on her checklist when they boarded the coach. She reserved a special smile of welcome for Joe who, typically, was last to climb aboard.

"I do believe the girl has the hots for him," Brenda commented as she and Sheila took the seats immediately behind their driver, the same seats they commandeered on most STAC outings.

"Jealous, dear?"

Brenda guffawed. "What? Of a young bimbo like that? You know what they say about not teaching old dogs new tricks, but that doesn't mean us old dogs can't teach young pups a thing or two."

Dressed in a pair of loose-fitting, tropical shorts, T-shirt and his inevitable gilet, Joe was carrying a large camera case, and as he settled into the seat across the aisle from his two companions, immediately behind Diana's jump seat, he stowed everything in the overhead rack.

A couple of rows back, Les Tanner felt obliged to comment. "For heaven's sake, Murray, did you have to bring all your luggage?"

"Proper camera, Les. You know. Like the one you had nicked in Cornwall?"

From across the aisle, Brenda drew his attention. "I'd have thought you had plenty of time to take pictures when you ran away from Palmanova."

"I did not run away from Palmanova. It was a tactical withdrawal."

Brenda grinned lasciviously. "Oh. You mean like when you pull out—"

"Brenda." Sheila's voice was heavy with threat. "This is a STAC outing. STAC not smut." She concentrated on Joe. "But like Brenda said, why didn't you take your pictures the last time you were here?"

"Because, if you remember, I legged it pretty sharpish from Palmanova, and you took my luggage home. My cameras were with my cases, and I wasn't about to get conned into buying a load of cheap rubbish from the traders here."

With the last of the passengers in their seats, Diana had a brief word with their driver, who returned a garrulous torrent of Spanish, and then started the engine. As the bus pulled away, Diana took up the PA microphone.

"Well, good morning, everybody. It's another beautiful day here on the reef, and we have an absolutely cracking tour ahead of us. We'll stop for coffee at a little town named Villaflor, up in the hills, and then beyond that, we'll have a brief stop at a well-known observation point where you can take photographs. From then, it will be up, up, and up to the plateau, the *Parque Nacional del Teide*. We'll park at the cable car station, the *Teléferico del Teide*, which is about nine hundred metres from the summit. If you want to take the cable car up to the peak, it'll cost you twenty-seven euros." Diana paused a moment, allowing them to take in her brief description and fluent Spanish, and then went on. "We'll have an hour or so there. Plenty of time for you to take photographs, grab a beer or a cup of coffee, and then we'll start back down, but with a stop at *Los Roques de Garcia*, an area famous for the bizarre shapes of the volcanic rocks, and we'll have about half an hour there for you to take even more photographs. After that, we'll start our descent towards the western coast of the island, and there'll be a final stop at a little place called Guia de Isora, where there's an absolutely fabulous perfume shop, and I know that you ladies will be itching to get at their special offers. For the gentleman, the place does sell beer."

The final announcement brought a ragged laugh from the passengers, and Diana settled into her jump seat, leaving her charges to their own devices.

Joe picked up *Smiley's People*, and immersed himself in its pages. Brenda plugged her mp3 player into her ears, and settled back with ABBA, while Sheila opened up a magazine.

Forty minutes later by which time Joe was beginning to tire of George Smiley, Madame Ostrakava, Toby Esterhase, and company, the bus pulled into a parking area opposite a small cafeteria on the outskirts of Villaflor, and everyone climbed off, grateful for the opportunity to stretch their legs as they made for the vacant tables.

Joe took his camera with him, and as he climbed from the bus, Diana assured him that from the tables at the rear of the café, they would normally be able to see a stretch of the Atlantic Ocean to the south, but a build-up of white, non-threatening cloud coming in from the African mainland, blotted the coast out.

Brenda ordered and paid for the coffees, and when they settled down with them, Joe fooling around with the lenses of his Sony DSLR, she glanced across at Diana, who was talking with Cyril Peck and Mavis Barker. The courier cast a glance in their direction and gave Brenda a smile.

Keeping her voice low, Brenda said, "You know she fancies you, don't you?"

Joe dragged his attention away from the intricacies of his camera, and looked over his shoulder. "Who? Mavis?" His wrinkled features twisted into a grimace of disgust.

"Not Mavis, you idiot. Diana. Our long-legged courier. You could be on there."

He gaped. "Have you taken leave of your senses? She's half my age. Young enough to be my granddaughter."

Sheila giggled. "Age is no barrier to true love, Joe."

He looked over his shoulder again. Diana smiled at him, and he delivered a crooked half smile by return. He turned back to his companions. "She'd kill me." A grin spread across his crinkly features. "Mind you, the undertaker would never get the smile off my face."

The two women dissolved into fits of quiet laughter, and when it dried up, Sheila's face became more serious.

"Problems?" Joe asked. He was concerned that the subtropical weather, the general holiday atmosphere was taking her back to the disaster which had been her honeymoon in the Cape Verde Islands.

"I was thinking of poor Tabitha this morning. I do hope she and Rodney are all right."

It was news to Joe, and he immediately demanded a full explanation. Brenda left it to her best friend, and while they finished their coffee, Sheila told him what had happened in the hotel reception.

Joe reacted with typical cynicism. "What were you saying about true love? Age might not be a barrier, but no matter how old you are, it still needs a good coating of tarmac to smooth the path. Tell you what, though. It explains that row we heard last night."

"Tabitha did say they'd had words." A frown crossed Sheila's brow. "She also said they were all right by bedtime, but he's switched his phone off this morning."

Joe was ready with an explanation. "He was probably feeling his oats last night, and—"

"Like someone else we know," Brenda cut in.

"Bog off, you. I was saying, he was probably feeling his oats last night, so pretended everything was lovely in the garden, then woke up this morning with the mood still on him." He finished his coffee. "Gar, what businesses is it of ours? Come on. Let's get back on the bus."

They left the little town just before eleven thirty, and from there the narrow road began to climb more steeply, through what amounted to a mountain path, precipitous, rocky cliffs on one side, a dizzying drop on the other, although occasionally, the seaward side was closed off with pine trees.

Twenty minutes after leaving the cafeteria, the driver pulled into an observation layby, and Diana took up the microphone.

"Okay, people, once we get off the bus, you will have a fantastic view right across the Atlantic Ocean, and in the distance, you'll see the island of Gran Canaria. We'll stop for about a quarter of an hour, just enough time for you to take pictures, and then we'll go on our way up to Teide."

Camera in hand, lenses attached, Joe was first off the bus, and looked out across the south eastern aspect of Tenerife. He could make out the coast, and some of the resorts. He could even see aircraft climbing into the sky from the airport, but looking out across the ocean, more of the same cloud which had blocked the view from Villaflor had built up, and he could see nothing of any other islands.

"So where the hell is Gran Canaria?"

Diana stood close at his shoulder and pointed. "Over there. That little black blob sticking up above the clouds."

His nostrils filled with Diana's perfume, conscious of Brenda's opinion of the girl, he followed her pointing finger to where he could just make out the uneven landscape, no more than a dark shape breaking through the cloud.

"I wouldn't have known if you hadn't pointed it out."

Alongside them, Brenda clicked away with her compact camera. "What did you expect, Joe? An arrow in the sky pointing down, and a large, illuminated sign saying, 'this is Gran Canaria'?"

"Something more interesting than that." Nevertheless, he put the camera to his eye, adjusted the telephoto lens, and pressed the button.

"Expensive tackle," Diana said as they made their way back to the coach.

"A few hundred quid. Clever piece of kit, too. I've got it set to take three separate images every time I press the button, and they're all slightly different in tone and colour."

"I'm impressed."

She climbed back on the bus, and Brenda sidled up alongside Joe. They watched Diana's shapely bottom climb up the steps, and Brenda whispered, "She's impressed with your tackle and you look impressed with her gearbox."

Joe looked at her. "Jealous?"

"Of her youth and figure, yes. Of her come and get it attitude, never. I'm surprised she doesn't hand out a price list to all the men."

"Like Tabby Wade?"

The narrow road wound and twisted its way up the steep climb, circling hairpin after hairpin, and when it swung to the left, they often found themselves looking down more vertiginous drops. Joe considered himself well travelled, especially around Great Britain, and he often considered some of the Pennine hills to be steep, but they were nothing compared to this. He found himself wondering what they would do if José, their driver, lost control.

"Stick your head between your knees and kiss your bottom goodbye, I suppose," Brenda said when he put the point to her.

For almost an hour they continued the steep climb, and gradually, the pine forest gave way to a more barren landscape. Rocky escarpments dominated the view on both sides. Diana built up the tension nicely, telling them that the first thing they would see would be the black river (a recent lava flow running down the western slopes) and then they would be confronted with Teide in all its majesty.

She was not wrong. The peak came upon them only gradually, but when it did, it was awe-inspiring; especially to people who came from a relatively low-lying country like Great Britain.

While the bus wound its way along the narrow road around the southern slopes and his fellow passengers gazed in wonder on the spectacle, Joe found himself framing shots in his mind. Teide from a distance, Teide close up, the bus in the foreground, with Teide in the background.

Most of them, he knew, would not happen. They would park at the cable car station, from where sightseers could go further up, but the peak would be hidden behind the higher slopes.

A quarter of an hour later, as José parked the bus, he found, to his disappointment, that he was right. The cable car lower station, almost 1,000 metres from the summit, was situated on one of the shallower climbs, but the hillside curved away from them leaving the peak invisible.

The station was a tarmac scar on the plateau. A small roundabout allowed coaches and cars to turn back, and all around the area was a low retaining wall, its concrete inner formed into a long, unbroken bench. The station itself was crowded, with many people waiting to board the *teléferico*, but when the two women asked, Joe declined with a wave of the hand which took in the general area.

"The air up here is thinner, and you know how bad my breathing is. If I go any higher, I'll need oxygen."

"It's nothing to do with the cost, then?"

Brenda's teasing was always easy to spot and Joe agreed with her spec analysis. "Twenty-seven euros for a one-kilometre ride up the hill is scandalous. Imagine the riots if the buses in Sanford charged that much. You two go, if you like. I'll stay here."

They, too, decided not to travel to the summit (or as near to the summit as the cable car would take them) and instead after securing hot drinks for themselves and a beer for Joe, they concentrated on the souvenir shop, while Joe took himself outside.

His comment on needing oxygen might have been intended as a joke, but there was no mistaking the difference between the coastal area and here on the plateau, which was at about 7,000 feet. Despite the sunshine, it was cooler, and Joe wished he had brought a jumper or a cardigan with him. His breathing felt better, but he attributed that to the cleaner, unpolluted air, and his concern was on a point his GP had once stressed to him. Cold air might feel better, but it was not always a good thing; it had the potential to cause a COPD flare-up.

He stood by the long, low wall, looking over the whole plateau. This area (so it was claimed) had been used for scenes in movies like *Star Wars* and the original *Planet of the Apes*, and it was easy to see why. The entire plateau looked alien. Cragged hills rose up around the rim at a distance of about three miles, stark spires jutted into the cloudless sky, and if that sky had been black rather than a spectacular blue, the area could be mistaken for the surface of the moon. Joe snapped away with his Sony, and as he checked the images on the camera's tiny screen, he debated whether they would make simple, album snaps, or whether they should be enlarged and printed on canvas, or a similar surface, and hung on the wall of The Lazy Luncheonette.

Kneeling on the seat, leaning over the wall he targeted a shot of *Los Roques de Garcia*, three kilometres to the south. The bus was scheduled to make a brief stop there on the way back, but a shot from here, with a 700mm zoom, would make a fine landscape, with a central focus: the best kind of panoramic shot. Behind him, he heard the whine of motors as the cable car set off on its eight minute climb to the summit, or brakes as the descending car approached the station. He looked up, and saw Alec and Julia Staines waving at him from the car. Quickly adjusting the focus of his camera, he turned and snapped them before they disappeared out of sight.

He began dismantling the camera, and Diana appeared at his side. "Got all your photographs?"

"Enough. I'll be taking a few more when we get down to wossname... the rocks."

"Los Roques. You've been before?"

Joe nodded and swallowed a mouthful of beer. "A few times. My wife lives in Las Américas."

Contrary to Brenda's opinion, Diana seemed surprised but not disappointed. "Your wife lives here and you're in England?"

"Sorry. My bad. I should have said ex-wife. She moved out here when we split up. We get on okay now, but that's probably because there's two thousand miles between us. What about you, Diana? You hitched?"

She delivered a throaty laugh. "Not likely. Young, footloose and fancy-free."

Joe chuckled. "Same here. Only not quite so young."

Quite abruptly she changed the subject, her face turning serious. "Word is you're some kind of private detective. You've been all over the local English papers in Las Américas."

He laughed again. "That kind of fame I could do without. Yes, I am a private detective, but it's strictly a sideline. I run a trucker's café in West Yorkshire."

"Ah. You're probably not the man I'm looking for then."

Joe was uncertain whether to feel relieved or disappointed, but over her shoulder he could see Brenda and Sheila approaching, and as they sat alongside Joe, it was obvious that they had overheard Diana's comment.

"You're looking for a man? They don't come any manlier than Joe Murray."

It seemed to Joe that Brenda's semi-humorous observation was marinated in resentment, but if so, Diana missed it.

"Oh, hello, Mrs Jump, Mrs Riley. I was just saying to Mr Murray that I'd read he was a private eye, but he's just told me he's a part timer."

"And a full-time pain in the posterior," Sheila commented. "Don't let him fool you, Diana. Joe is one of the best. Is there something you need to talk to him about? Boyfriend trouble, perhaps?"

Diana laughed harshly. "Hell, no. I live in Las Américas. I can get all the boyfriends I want."

Brenda shrugged. "In that case, luv, you really are looking at the wrong man. As boyfriends go, he's brilliant at making steak and kidney pudding, but—"

Joe interrupted. "Shall we get back on the bus?"

Chapter Twelve

"I really must thank you for that vote of confidence."

Ensuring Diana was out of earshot, checking on the passengers as they arrived, Joe made his sarcastic remark as they climbed back on the bus half an hour later.

Brenda took her seat next to Sheila, Joe dropped his camera bag on the empty seat beside him, and settled in.

Pulling the safety belt around her midriff, Brenda challenged him. "If she's in some kind of trouble, Joe, the last thing she needs is you. She'd need someone close to her age, someone likely to understand the kind of problems that generation has. Anyway, you're on holiday."

He took his time thinking about it. "I do understand young people. I gave that Nadia a job after Squire's Lodge."

"Diana's not Nadia. And anyway, Nadia was a waste of space. She left in less than a month. Joe, I'm only trying to stop you making a fool of yourself."

"You don't stop to think about when you two are making a fool of me."

"We're entitled," Sheila said. "We're your best friends. We're not just after your wallet or getting you to work for nothing."

Joe would have challenged them further, but the final passengers – Alec and Julia Staines –climbed onto the bus, followed by Diana. José started the engine, turned the vehicle round, and set off back down the hill. At the junction with the main road, the TF-21, he took a sharp right as if he were making his way back to Villaflor and Playa de Las Américas. A couple of miles on the road, he turned right again, onto a long, straight stretch, a cul-de-sac, at the end of which was a large turning circle. José turned the coach round, tucked it in on the right, and Diana took up the microphone once more.

"Okay, folks, this is *Los Roques de Garcia*. We have half an hour here for photographs, and then we'll be on our way."

Joe, his camera slung over his shoulder, was first off the bus. It was a familiar arrangement. No matter where they went, at home or abroad, he would always wait to assist the more elderly members off the coach.

With Diana stood alongside him, he queried her. "So what kind of problems are you having that would need a private investigator?"

"I'm not actually looking for anyone, Mr Murray. All I need is someone who might be able to do a bit of negotiating for me. I'm sorry if I've upset you."

"No, no. I'm not upset. Just puzzled. Like the girls said, as detectives go, I'm the best, and when it comes to negotiating, they don't come any tougher than me." Helping Irene Pyecock from the coach, he waved around them. "I'm the one who haggled the price down on this holiday… Think about it."

When everyone had vacated the coach, Joe, Sheila and Brenda ambled towards the turning circle, from where they had a grandstand view of the spectacular rock formations and Teide in the background. Renowned as one of the major attractions in the area, the strange and bizarre leftovers of previous eruptions bore familiar names: The Finger of God, pointing like an index finger into the sky, The Thumb of God, a stack of rocks, resting on the narrowest of foundations.

After taking a couple of photographs of the rocks, with the peak of Teide in the middle, he handed the camera to Brenda and asked her to take a photograph of him stood before the formations. Afterwards, he took similar photographs of her, then Sheila, followed by an image of the two women stood together. Other members of the 3rd Age Club drew close, and Joe grouped them altogether, before handing his camera to Diana, telling her how to operate it, and joining them for a final photograph.

"That'll go on the wall of The Lazy Luncheonette," he declared after checking the image on the camera's screen.

Some of the members decided to climb the steps up into the rock formations, but as with the *teléferico*, Joe and his companions decided against it, and took a seat on a low wall not far from the coach, basking in the sunshine.

Joe rolled a cigarette as Diana joined them.

"Do you get sick of it?" Sheila asked as the young woman sat alongside them. "You know. Taking people on this same trip time after time. It must get boring."

"Not really. It's always different people, and to be honest, I love living here. What was the weather like when you left Manchester?"

"Freezing cold and legging it down."

Joe's comment caused Diana to laugh. "I think we had a short shower in February." She concentrated on Sheila. "See what I mean?"

Brenda was obviously still mistrustful of Diana. "So come on, what's this about you needing Joe or a reasonable facsimile?"

The younger women sighed. "It's nothing, Mrs Jump. Seriously. I'll sort it out myself."

Joe frowned. "Whatever it is, you obviously feel you need someone, or you wouldn't have brought it up. Listen, Diana, we run one of the busiest cafés in Yorkshire. We're privy to all sorts of gossip, but secrecy, keeping our mouths shut, is part of our stock in trade. Tell us what the score is, and even if we can't help, we might be able to suggest something."

Once more, she sighed. "I owe money."

Sheila tutted, and Brenda chuckled. "You're knocking on the wrong door, luv. Joe's wallet not only has a padlock, but a twelve-digit, alphanumeric combination lock."

Now Joe huffed out his breath and took an exasperated drag on his cigarette. "I really must get you to work on my public image, Brenda." He turned to Diana. "A lot of money?"

"Five hundred euros. Not a lot to you, maybe, but on my wages, it's a serious problem." She fired a darting glance Brenda. "Before you ask, Mrs Jump, I'm not looking to borrow any money. I'm looking for someone to try and get the guy I owe to back off. Not easy, but for the right man, it wouldn't be impossible." She honed her eyes on Joe. "According to the reports in the local papers, you might be the right kind of man because you're ready to take a risk."

Sheila promptly disagreed. "There are risks and risks, dear. Joe doesn't deal with loan sharks."

"This isn't a loan shark, Mrs Riley. It's Ken Lowfield. Him what owns The Mother's Ruin." Other passengers were slowly making their way back to the coach, and Diana spotted them. "You'll have to excuse me. Duty calls."

"Granted," Joe said. "But when we get to Isadora's perfume factory, I'll only be having a quick cuppa, so you can tell me all about it there."

From *Los Roques*, the road twisted and turned on its way across the plateau, sometimes running north, then west, then south and east, passing through rock gorges and pine forests, sometimes with spectacular views of Teide or the open expanse of the Atlantic, but as they drove on, Joe became more and more nervy. He had made this journey before, and somewhere, not too far ahead, they would have to descend from the 7,000 feet of the plateau, to sea level. It was, as he recalled, an unnerving experience. If José lost control, they would all be doomed.

Several miles further on, their driver made a sharp left turn onto a narrow road leading down to the village of Ghiguergue. Joe's faith in their driver was limited, but José soon demonstrated his skill, dropping the vehicle into a low gear, and allowing the engine's natural retard to control his speed as they negotiated the tight, twisting bends.

Joe noticed his ears blocking as they carried on down the steep incline, but a quarter of an hour later, the road levelled off, and he breathed a sigh of relief as José took the winding, twisting, TF-82 to the town of Guia de Isora, and almost immediately pulled onto the parking area outside the perfume outlet.

Diana gave her usual speech of allowing thirty minutes to an hour for the passengers to sample the delights of the shop and the cafeteria, before everyone climbed off the coach.

"We'll find you some nice aftershave, Joe," Sheila promised, and he made his way to the cafeteria practically dragging Diana with him.

It was an open plan establishment, the cafeteria taking up one corner of the room, while all around were shelves of souvenirs, and locally produced perfumes, but behind the cash desk, Joe noticed they also sold more expensive scents: brand names like Chanel, Hugo Boss, L'Oreal, et al.

Securing coffee and cakes, he sat with their guide, and invited her to help herself from the plate of fancies. She declined, and Joe went straight on the attack.

"Tell me about Ken Lowfield."

"Well, Mr Murray, it's not really my place—"

He cut her off. "Stop fannying about, Diana. You owe him money, you say he's not a loan shark. So what is he?" Doubt was there to be read in her face and he had to press further. "See, I worked for Paddy McLintock for a while, back when he owned The Mother's Ruin. And I remember Paddy telling me that he would never go back to England. According to Lowfield, he's done just that. Then there's been arguments between Lowfield and young Spike Wade, who, incidentally, has gone missing this morning, and now I find that you owe him money, and he's obviously pressing you to pay up. Now come on. What's going down?"

She sighed and nibbled at an iced fancy. "Card sharking, Mr Murray."

"Please. Call me Joe. What d'you mean, card sharking? According to my ex-wife, Lowfield plays cards regularly with a bloke called Harry Givens, and also the guy what owns Laurel's on the front of the hotel."

She nodded. "He does. Poker, mainly. And they're good; him and Manny. They win more than they lose. Anyway, I got involved in a game one night, didn't I? I thought it was just a bit of fun, picked up a hand with three aces, and I thought, yes, I'm on a winner here. I lost. Lowfield turned up with something called a straight. Taught me a lesson, I can tell you. I came away owing him five hundred euros, and to be honest, I don't have it. I don't get paid a fantastic amount on this job, but I'm happy with what I have. He gave me a fortnight to come up with the money. That was ten days ago." Tears began to sparkle in her eyes. "I'm getting desperate. I have to find that money within four days. You don't know what he's like. If I don't pay, he'll arrange for someone to beat it out of me. I mean it. He's an absolute nut job like that."

Joe chewed his lip and recalled the incident with Spike Wade on Sunday evening. "Not much I can say, Diana, other than don't be such a bloody fool in future. Guys like him, and possibly Manny at Laurel's, don't play for fun." He racked his mind for an angle. "Are they kosher? You know. On the level? They're not cheating?"

Diana shrugged. "How would I know? I was drunk at the time... Well, half cut. What made it worse was, I won a few hands before they upped the ante. I should have walked away, but I don't think they'd have let me. All along they kept saying, 'come on, Diana, give us a chance to win our money back'. I should have walked away."

Joe sipped his coffee and ate a small Battenberg. It gave him another opportunity to clear his thinking. "It sounds like a bog-standard scam, to me. They draw you in, let you win a few, and then hit you. And you're only guilty of being naïve. Do you know what happened to Paddy? Why he sold up?"

Diana shrugged. "Your ex-wife would be the one to know that. She's worked there for years, hasn't she?"

His eyebrows rose. "You know Alison? Only earlier, it sounded like you didn't."

"I do know her, yes. Not well, but all the Brits in that area know one another. If you wanna find out about Ken and what happened to Paddy, try asking Ali."

As they finished their coffee, Sheila and Brenda joined them with fresh cups, and Brenda placed a small bag, marked with the establishment's logo, in front of Joe. "There you go, boss. We've brought you some alcohol-free aftershave."

"Alcohol free?"

Brenda grinned. "Well the bottle actually says, *sin alcohol*, so maybe it isn't alcohol free. Maybe it's fifty proof. That should be enough for a bit of sinning, shouldn't it?"

"I want to slap it on my cheeks, not drink it."

Diana laughed. "*Sin alcohol* is Spanish for alcohol-free, Joe. You can splash this on, and it won't sting."

Joe grunted. "Trust me, when you've worked with these two as long as I have, the sting of aftershave is a positive pleasure."

Brenda took one of the fancies from Joe's plate, and wolfed it down. "So, did you get any further?"

"Yes, and it doesn't make for pleasant reading." He focused on Diana. "The best I can do for you, chicken, is have a word with Lowfield. I don't know that it'll do any good, but I'll speak to him after I've spoken to Alison."

Diana shook her head. "Talking won't do no good, Mr Murray. What it needs is someone to take him on at his own game. Someone who knows what they're doing. I thought with you being a private detective, you'd be into all that kind of thing. They always are in the movies, aren't they?"

"I'm not a movie star." Joe screwed up his face again. "I don't play cards. I never won at happy families, never mind poker. I don't even understand the game."

Sheila's face became a mask of concern. "What on earth is going on?"

"I've told you, it doesn't make for pleasant listening. I'll clue you up in a little while, but if I'm right, Ken Lowfield is a scammer of the first magnitude."

His mood now sombre, disturbed, he glanced at the glorious sunshine through the windows, and almost immediately his eyes fell upon Tabby Wade arguing with Harry Givens, and this time, there was no mistaking their identities.

He half rose, but as he did so, Tabby jumped into a black Seat, started the engine and tore away. With a sad shake of the head, Givens climbed into his hired car, a Fiat 500, and drove off after her.

Joe's voice was a murmur, speaking to himself. "Now what the hell is going on there?"

Chapter Thirteen

While they waited for the straggle of passengers to get back to the coach, Joe brought his two companions up to speed on the things Diana had told him.

Brenda wasted no time thinking about it. "I don't know where she gets the idea that you could take on card sharks. Even if you knew what you were doing, Joe, it could be a dangerous game."

"And you think that hadn't already occurred to me?" Joe rolled another cigarette and lit it. "Tell you what, though, Owen Frickley reckons he's better than scratch at poker."

Sheila tutted. "He might be, but that's not the solution. I don't approve of gambling, but if we're going to help this poor girl out of a spot, we need to negotiate, not take on Ken Lowfield at his own game."

Joe hastened to correct her. "That's not what I was thinking. I was thinking if Owen took him on, won a good dip off him, then we could negotiate. Give this chicken time to pay, or we will send Owen in again and clean him out."

Both women had their doubts, and the debate petered out.

It was a few minutes after four when the bus finally pulled away from the perfume factory. José backtracked a little, to drop onto the main motorway, TF-1, from where, Diana assured them, it would take less than half an hour back to the Torviscas Atoll.

Brenda, her bags typically full of purchases, nodded off to sleep within minutes of the bus's departure, while Sheila, her magazine abandoned, examined her booty of perfumes and sprays. Across the aisle from them, Joe was beginning to feel the strain of the day, and needed some sleep, but he could not help thinking about the things he had learned, specifically concerning Paddy McLintock, Ken Lowfield and the fate of

The Mother's Ruin.

From the brief description Diana had given him, and observations of having Givens passing money to Manuel a couple of days previously, he guessed that the pub landlord and restaurateur were in league, pulling some kind of scam, but he knew next to nothing about card games. He recalled a trip to Las Vegas some years previously, and he had watched at the blackjack and poker tables, and while he understood the basics, he didn't really have a clue who was winning and losing.

Worse, the only two people who might have understood, George Robson and Owen Frickley, had chosen not to come with them on this trip. He made a mental note to have a word with them when he got back to the Atoll, and somewhere along the line, he would need a word with Alison, see what she could tell him.

The single thought of his ex-wife turned his entire attention to her, Diana's problems forgotten for the moment.

If both were older, wiser than when they first met and married, the previous night had seen a return to those early passions, albeit tempered with advancing years, and Brenda could be forgiven for suggesting that a reconciliation might be on the cards. Joe knew differently. There was a cosmic gulf between them.

Yorkshire born and raised Alison might have been, but she was now an expat, a dedicated Canary Islander, and nothing short of compulsory repatriation on the part of the Spanish government (which would never happen in a millennium plus one) would persuade her to return to England.

Joe was exactly the opposite. He understood the attraction and temptation of Tenerife, and he had no doubt that life here would be more convivial than West Yorkshire, but as Ken Lowfield had pointed out on the afternoon of their arrival, business pressures, the urgent need to make a living, would be no different. In addition, there was too much about the old country, life in Sanford, that he would miss, even if some of those aspects irritated more than pleased him.

He and Alison were destined to be no more than good

friends and holiday lovers, but even so, his philosophy decreed that it was preferable to the bitterness between them when they first separated.

He remembered few of the arguments, but he remembered what they were about; work. Alison was no slouch (she wouldn't be working at The Mother's Ruin if she were) but she needed her time off, and she did not count hanging around the flat above the old Lazy Luncheonette as a day off. As a businessman, moreover a one-man band, Joe had no choice but to work, and he settled for free time during breaks such as this and the frequent 3rd Age Club excursions to one place or another.

According to Brenda, the signs had been there virtually from the day they married, when Alison attempted to impose early closing on the café. Joe would not have it. He had been behind the counter since his schooldays, and he knew the place. Closing at two o'clock would lose valuable custom late in the afternoon, particularly when schoolchildren were making their way home.

Whatever the rights and wrongs of their marriage and subsequent divorce, Joe was pleased that they could settle into a solid, even intimate, friendship while he was here, and he actively looked forward to seeing her again before the week was out.

José pulled up outside the main entrance to the Atoll just after half past four, and it was a tired contingent of passengers who climbed off, straggled into the hotel, making for their rooms, and Joe noticed with approval that most of them dropped coins into the little basket their driver positioned within arm's reach of the steering wheel. When the last of the passengers descended, he hopped back up onto the bus, handed José a ten-euro note and in pidgin Spanish, thanked him for the day's outing.

As he stepped off the coach once more, the searing heat of a Tenerife afternoon hit him like a sledgehammer and waves of fatigue swept over him. After a brief word with Diana, he ambled back into the hotel, made his way to his room, and once there, stripped down to his underwear, flopped onto the bed, and in minutes he was asleep…

A kind of dusk enveloped the bedroom when he woke up. A quick check on his phone revealed the time at half past six. Rolling from the mattress, he felt thoroughly invigorated, refreshed, renewed, ready for anything the evening might throw at him.

He showered, shaved, and dressed, putting on the familiar fawn-coloured trousers, a pale blue, white and lemon patchwork shirt, and his comfortable loafers. Once ready, he made a cup of tea and sat out on the balcony, watching the sun dip towards the ocean. It was exactly the same routine as he had carried out the previous evening, and he was happy to do so again, for no other reason than he found it so relaxing. In the past, he had always been sceptical of people's fascination with the subject, especially coastal sunsets. Painters – some of them anyway – seemed to be obsessed with them, and he could never understand why. Three days sitting on this balcony, watching the sun metaphorically settle into the Atlantic, had changed his mind. He felt more at peace now than at any other time he could remember.

It would not last. As he drank his tea, blue flashing lights reflecting from the upper floor of The Mother's Ruin drew his attention. He stood up to look over the balcony wall, and saw Lowfield handcuffed and struggling with two police officers. Even as they tried to pressure him into the rear of their vehicle, he put his foot on the rear step, and pushed back at them. His resistance was nothing more than furious futility. They bundled him into the small van, slammed and locked the door, climbed into the front and drove away. While Joe continued watching, patrons began to file out of the bar, two officers remained on duty to ensure no one went back in, and finally, Mariella Lowfield emerged and was pleading with another policeman, this one bearing the epaulettes of a senior officer. Whoever he was, he gesticulated frantically at Mariella and then, leaving the two sentries behind, climbed into his car and drove away. Alison was last out of the place, and she took Mariella gently by the hand, and led her to a vacant table.

Joe drank his tea. "No rest for the wicked, lad."

He had arranged to meet Sheila and Brenda in reception at eight o'clock, from where they would amble down to the *centro comercial* for their evening meal, but his natural curiosity compelled him to cross the road to the bar to find out what had been going off.

Was it serendipity or synchronicity? He could never remember the difference between the two, but just a couple of hours previously he had been talking with Diana, concerned with Lowfield's potential as a cheat at cards, and now here was the proprietor of The Mother's Ruin under arrest. Had Diana been talking to the police? Had someone else complained about shady practices? It all seemed too much to be coincidence.

He never got as far as The Mother's Ruin before he learned what was going on, and it was more serious than he first thought.

When he reached the lobby, he found Tabby Wade in a flood of tears, her upper body racking with sobs. She was attended by Pablo and Nina, while at the desk another clerk was on the phone, presumably to Diana.

When Joe joined them Nina was the first to speak and although she was fluent in English, she spoke in her native tongue.

"*Señor Wade. Muerto.*"

Joe's Spanish was limited, but he needed no interpreter to work out what the receptionist meant. He got straight on the phone to Sheila.

"I'm in reception and we have a crisis down here. Tabby Wade is in a hell of a state and she could do with some support."

"What's happened, Joe?"

"Spike. From what I gather, he's dead."

"Oh, dear lord. We're on our way."

Joe slipped the phone back into his pocket as the connection died, and wormed his way in, to sit alongside Tabby. He took her hand and she leaned into his shoulder, weeping uncontrollably.

"He murdered Spike."

Joe patted her hand. "Sure." He glanced up at Pablo and Nina. "Sheila and Brenda are on their way down. They're better at this than me."

He did not know whether they understood him, whether they knew what he was talking about. His futility, helplessness and guilt (he always felt guilty when confronted with women who cried, even when he had no reason to feel guilty) would transmit itself to the locals.

He focussed on the distraught woman again. "Who killed him, Tabby?"

"Him." She waved hysterically at the outside world. "Ken bloody Lowfield."

Without knowing if she was right or wrong, it made a sort of sense. Lowfield might be guilty, he might not be, but the police had obviously taken him away for further questioning, albeit not without a struggle, and if he was innocent, why would he try to fight them off?

To his relief, Sheila and Brenda arrived, and while Brenda took over the task of comforting Tabby, Joe gave Sheila a rundown of the minimal information he had.

"You look after her. I'll be back soon."

"Where are you going?"

Already making his way to the exit, Joe nodded at the outside world. "Mother's Ruin. See what I can find out."

The heat of the evening hit him, and as he made his way across the four-lane, dual carriageway, consciously reminding himself to look in the direction opposite to home, he thought idly about the cost of running air-conditioning virtually all year round. He complained about the energy bills for his house, but at least he could leave the central heating off during the summer months.

Alison and Mariella were sat outside, both had a drink (it looked like brandy to Joe) set on the table before them, and Mariella, similar to Tabby, was mopping up tears with a tissue while Ali comforted her.

"Thank God you're here," Ali greeted him. "I was gonna bring Mariella over to the Atoll when she calmed down."

"Not a good idea. Tabby Wade is over there, and she's blaming Ken. Better to keep them apart." Joe sat down, picked up Ali's glass, and took a sip of neat brandy. "Bloody hell. That needs a bit of lemonade or something in it."

"Yes, well, the police won't let us back in the bar, not even for the drop of lemonade or ginger ale. Not until their forensic people are finished, and that won't be until tomorrow at the earliest."

"So where's Mariella gonna stay tonight?"

"My place. You know the score, Joe. I put you up for long enough, didn't I?"

"Hang fire while I nip next door and pick up a can of cola. You want anything, either of you?"

"The lemonade you mentioned would be good."

Joe hurried from the table and down the street to the English chippy next door, when he bought three cans of soft drink, and hurried back to The Mother's Ruin.

He cracked the can of cola, and drank gratefully, quenching his thirst, combating the hot bite of the brandy he had swallowed a few minutes earlier.

Alison took one can of lemonade, opened it, poured some into her glass, and topped up Mariella's.

When they were settled, Joe played his standard opening move. "Okay, tell me what happened. I know Spike Wade has been found dead. Pablo and Nina told me that much, and as I said, Tabby is blaming Ken. Fill in the gaps."

Alison looked to Mariella, who spoke in rapid Spanish. Her English was better than adequate, but in the interest of expediency, it was better that she spoke in her native tongue, allowing Alison to translate, reminding Joe that after many years of residency, his ex-wife was fluent.

"What I'm telling you, Joe, is third hand. The police say they found Rod Wade's body earlier this evening." Alison pointed across the street to the Atoll. "He'd been dumped in the hotel's underground car park, and from what they're saying, he was beaten to death. They made enquiries at the Atoll's reception, and soon identified him. From there they spoke to his wife, Tabitha, and she blamed Ken. They came across here, there was a bit of a debate, and... Well, you've seen what Ken's like. He took a poke at the man in charge, and they carted him off to the local nick."

Joe sucked in more cola. "And they think he did it?"

Once again, it was Mariella who spoke, delivering a torrent of Spanish which, married to her outrage features, told Joe all he needed to know without interpretation.

Alison translated it anyway. "He admitted to the scrap on Sunday evening. Wasn't much point denying it, really. The pub was crowded, and hundreds of people saw it, including you. But Mariella insists that he never saw or spoke to Wade after he threw him out. And I believe him, Joe. All right, Ken's a snapper. We all know that. But he's no killer, and if he did get into a second rumble with Spike Wade, he wouldn't have gone too far. He'd have knuckled the lad a couple of times, and left it at that."

"Do you think the cops will talk to me?"

Alison shrugged again. "You're a bit of a celebrity here, Joe, but that doesn't mean to say Inspector Vargas will let you get to Ken. All I can say is, try. At worst, Vargas will tell you to clear off."

"It'll be tomorrow morning before I get to them, but in the meantime, you should know that I've heard allegations against Ken."

"Cheating at cards?"

Joe nodded. "And that's what Sunday's argument was about, wasn't it? Nothing to do with Harry Givens, but everything to do with Ken and Manny at Laurel's ripping punters off in a game of poker."

"That's twaddle. We all know Ken and Manny play poker, and for money, and Givens joins them regular. But they don't cheat."

Joe frowned at Alison's reply. "So why was Spike having a go at Harry on Sunday night?"

Mariella smiled bleakly and Alison could only shrug once more while her employer's wife answered in Spanish.

Ali translated again. "Ken never told Mariella what it was about, but she thinks that Wade might have accused Givens of trying to pull his wife. Nothing to do with cheating at cards."

"And you insist Manny and Lowfield don't cheat?" Joe did not wait for an answer. "They took five ton off young Diana, the hotel rep, and she says Ken is threatening her. Pay up or else."

Alison laughed. "Dateless Diana? She's a nice enough kid, Joe, but she doesn't have two brain cells to rub together. And there's no way Ken took five hundred off her. She's his niece."

Joe buried an immediate flash of anger. "Then why did she —"

Alison cut him off. "She touts for him, looking for punters willing to take him on at poker. She tells them all sorts of porkies to get them into the game, and Ken pays her a percentage of his winnings. She also works behind the bar here a couple of nights a week. She'd have been on tonight if the cops had let us open."

"Wait while I see her."

Alison chuckled again. "Keep your cool, Joe. She's a holiday rep, and a fairly new one at that. Do you know how much they get paid? If she's on seven grand a year she's doing well, and like any other young lass, she's always short of money."

"And she gets a percentage of his winnings, huh? Guaranteed winnings?"

"I told you, Joe, Ken and Manny don't cheat."

Calming down, reserving his opinion, Joe drank more cola. "One last thing and I'll let you get on your way home with Mariella. Do you have a contact number for Paddy McLintock?"

The moment he said it, Mariella's face screwed up in puzzlement, and she unleashed a torrent of Spanish on Alison who listened, and then translated.

"You're thinking that Paddy lost The Mother's Ruin in a crooked card game?"

Joe lied. "It's been suggested."

"Well, it's wrong. For the last time, Ken and Manny don't

cheat. Paddy was a long-termer on the island, and he always said he would never go home, but his mother took seriously ill. Or, at least, that's what he told us. Ken made an offer for the bar, and he took it. Paddy was out of here within forty-eight hours of receiving the news, and left it to local lawyers to sort out the rest of the deal. I'll give him a bell, Joe, and leave your number with him. If he wants to get in touch with you, he will."

Chapter Fourteen

Tabby was still broken and weeping when Joe returned to the Atoll to find Sheila and Brenda sat with her in the reception area.

He spent a few minutes telling them what he had learned across the street, and then pointed out the obvious. "We all need to eat, but we can't leave her like this."

If he had taken bets on who would respond, his money would have been on Sheila, and he was right.

"Someone needs to stay with her. Brenda and I will take her back to the apartment, then you and Brenda nip out, get a meal, and when you come back I'll get something from the hotel's restaurant."

"If you want to play that way, it's better if you go first, Sheila. The hotel restaurant shuts at nine. Brenda and I can always nip across to the chippy over the road."

They agreed, and Joe accompanied them back up to Tabby's apartment, and once they put the young woman to bed, Brenda switched on the television and began channel hopping for British programmes, and Sheila left.

Joe made himself comfortable on the balcony, but to his disappointment found that it overlooked the motorway and the rugged hills behind the hotel. He nevertheless settled at the table, rolled and lit a cigarette, took out his phone, and dialled.

The connection took many seconds before the line began to ring out, and when Gemma Cradock answered, it was with a mixture of surprise and irritation.

"Uncle Joe? I thought you were on holiday, and I've clocked off for the day."

"I'm in Tenerife, but I need you to do me a favour,

Gemma."

With all the contempt born of familiarity, fully aware of what was going on, she groaned. "For God's sake, Joe, can't you mind your own business even when you're on holiday?"

He chuckled into the deepening night. "You know me, and to be honest, everything's hit the fan here. I need some information, and you're the only person I can think of who might be able to get it for me."

"Obviously. Because I'm next in line to the Home Secretary, aren't I? What do you want?"

"Detective Inspector Harry Givens. He comes from the Burnley area. Now we've just had a young kid killed here, and he comes from the same area. Spike Wade... Correction. Rodney Wade. There is something odd going on between Wade, Givens, and Wade's wife. I thought if you could make a few discreet enquiries and get back to me, I might be able to help sort it out."

Gemma sighed once more. "Why don't you leave it to the local police?"

"Because I think it's a lot more complicated than the Spanish plod realise. They've already walled someone up for it, and I'm waiting for the low down on him from another source. All I need to know from you is the score with Harry Givens."

There was a pause, and Joe could imagine her writing down the information. "Okay. Leave it with me, but it'll be tomorrow before I get back to you... at the earliest" Another pause followed. "Aside from sticking your oar in, are you having a good time?"

"Brilliant. Even better now I've a murder to investigate."

Gemma chuckled. "What am I gonna do with you?"

"Say thank you when I bring you a little souvenir of Tenerife."

With a wry smile Joe bade his niece goodnight, cut the connection and tossed the phone on the table. Relighting his cigarette, he took a deep drag, let the smoke out with a satisfied hiss and stared into the starlit night.

The only lighting came from the motorway below, and that

was sparse. Other than that, he could see occasional speckles on the inland hills, isolated farmhouses, tiny hamlets nestling on those rugged cliffs. And above them, the stars.

Even as a child he had looked up at the heavens and wondered about them, but Sanford was a heavy industrial area, and light pollution took its toll on the number of stars visible. From the rear of The Lazy Luncheonette, he could see nothing of the glory of the view from the balcony.

Like everything else about this island, he found it calming, relaxing, conducive to the marshalling of his thoughts.

"Gemma?"

Brenda's voice, cutting into his meditation, stirred him. "Hmm? What? Oh. Yes. How's Tabby?"

"Sleeping. The doctor gave her some kind of sedative." Carrying a cup of tea, Brenda settled into the chair alongside him. "Gemma?"

Joe puffed on his cigarette again. "She's a bit annoyed with me."

"I should think so too. Pestering her when you're two thousand miles from home. Joe, it's fairly obvious what happened. There was an argument between Spike and Lowfield on Sunday night. Spike must have hassled him again, and this time, Lowfield went too far."

"Except that according to Ali and Mariella, that's not what happened."

She sighed and took a sip of tea. "Mariella is his wife. What would you expect her to say? And as for Ali… It's none of my business, Joe, but you and she are getting pretty cosy."

"Envious?"

"Don't be childish." She put her cup on the table and like Joe, glanced up at the heavens before bringing her attention back to the here and now. "What happened to Sheila was enough to put me off permanent relationships for the rest of my life. I'm making an observation, Joe. I still remember when you and Ali split up. You always say there was no real aggro, but there was. Plenty of it."

"We're older and wiser."

"Well, older certainly."

"Brenda—"

She cut him off. "Joe, what you and Ali get up to is nothing to do with anyone, least of all me, but you can't just take her word on this. Mariella is defending her husband, Ali works for them, of course she'll take their side, but was she there when Spike was beaten to death? Was Mariella there? The police have arrested him, and that means they have evidence. You don't."

"I have a gut feeling, and that's enough for me." Joe crushed out the cigarette, and promptly began to roll another. "Ever since we got here, I've noticed things going on between Spike, Tabby and Harry Givens. I don't know what it's about, but it suggests a bigger motive for murder than any argument with Ken Lowfield."

"So what are you gonna do about it?"

"Talk to George Robson and Owen Frickley first thing tomorrow morning. And then I'm going down to the police station to see if the cops'll let me speak to Lowfield."

Brenda was about to take another mouthful from her cup. She changed her mind and put it back on the table. "George and Owen? A couple of Sanford scroats. What will they know about it?"

"Nothing. But Owen fancies his chances as a card sharp. We talked about it before, didn't we? If anyone knows anything about Ken Lowfield, and possibly Spike Wade, and even Harry Givens, and cheating at cards it'll be Owen."

"As I understood it, you'd already decided that Lowfield is a cheat."

"Ali and Mariella deny it. I think it's true, but before I confront Lowfield, I need to know one way or the other, and Owen is our best bet."

"I don't wanna be a wet blanket, but before you can confront Lowfield, you'll need the police's permission."

"That won't be a problem." He grinned. "You know me better than anyone, Brenda, and you know I'll persuade them."

The evening dragged on. The conversation varied from the immediate crisis, to the general ambience of life both in

Sanford and here on the island of Tenerife. Sheila returned at half past nine, after dining with Les Tanner and Sylvia Goodson. The conversation there had been livelier than in the Wade's apartment. After receiving a full run down on the scuttlebutt from her, Joe and Brenda left, making their way from the hotel across the road to the fish and chip shop next door to The Mother's Ruin.

It was a simple enough meal, sitting at tables outside the serving area, basking in the evening heat, the conversation as generalised as it had been in the hotel room. Joe complimented the proprietor on the quality of her tea, and she explained that she was originally from Derbyshire, and that she used imported teabags. She held up a catering-sized pack of Taylor's Yorkshire Tea, and he once again congratulated her on her taste.

Forty-five minutes after arriving there, they were about to leave, call at the hotel bar for a nightcap, when Joe's mobile rang. He checked the menu window. An unknown number, but with a prefix signalling a call from Great Britain. Thinking it might be Gemma, he made the connection and put the phone to his ear.

"You got back quicker than I expected, girl."

"Ali said it was important, and I'm not a girl. At least, I wasn't the last time I checked."

Joe recognised the voice of Paddy McLintock, and laughed aloud. "Sorry, Paddy, I was expecting a call from my niece."

Paddy laughed too. "The copper from Sanford?"

"The very same."

"So how are you, you miserable old twonk?"

Paddy's question caused Joe to laugh again. "Still miserable and enjoying life all the more for it. How about you?"

Paddy's gloom shone through his voice. "Truth is, mate, I miss life on the reef. How's the weather? Blazing sunshine, I suppose."

"Wall-to-wall," Joe agreed.

Paddy snorted. "Pi… Raining like hell here."

A few more minutes of reminiscence followed, Joe explaining how he had coped after his return to the UK, and Paddy bemoaning his downfall since he went home to Nottingham. Eventually Joe had had enough of the small talk.

"Did Ali tell you what's going on?"

"Part of it. Ken Lowfield's been arrested for murder or something."

"Spot on. We've been here four days and I keep getting conflicting tales about certain people, Ken Lowfield amongst them. One whisper is you lost The Mother's Ruin to him in a hooky game of cards."

Paddy laughed. "No chance. It was all above board, Joe. Truth of the matter is, my old queen took ill. My mother. There was no one to look after her, so I jumped on a plane and came home, and once I got here I knew I wouldn't be able to go back. She's too old and frail. I can't leave her. So I rang Kenny, told him what's what and asked if he fancied buying the bar from me. Course, he screwed the price down to the ground, but I came away with my nose in front. And now, I'm being the good son, looking after my mother between putting in shifts at a local bar, and the missus keeps an eye on Ma while I'm out working."

Joe did not know whether to be pleased or disappointed. "So you never played cards with Lowfield and Manny over at Laurels?"

"Nope. Not my scene, as you should know."

"You won't have heard the rumours then that they cheat?"

"Course I have. Everyone's heard those rumours, but there's no proof. Never has been. And trust me, even if it were true, I'm the last bloke Ken Lowfield and Manny Ibarra would cheat. I'd have battered them all over the island." There was a brief pause. "So who is Ken supposed to have murdered?"

"Holidaymaker. They were on the same flight as our mob. It's all a bit up and down, Paddy, but there's another bloke involved – I think – fella by the name of Harry Givens."

"Copper from Burnley. He's a regular on the island. Has

been for years. He used to favour Kenny's Bar down the town centre, but that's because Ken owned the place. Ali told me he's in The Mother's Ruin more than enough these days."

Joe chuckled. "Maybe I should listen to my ex-wife more."

"Better yet, maybe you should move to Tenerife and ship in with your ex-wife." Paddy responded quickly to Joe's laughter. "No, I mean it, mate. You were a brilliant, short order cook, and if you opened your own place there, you'd make a fortune."

"Yeah, and we had this discussion last time I was here, didn't we? Ali and I get on okay, but I'm in no rush to go back to the manacles of matrimony. Listen, Paddy, thanks for ringing. I'll have a word with the local plod tomorrow, see if I can't speak to Lowfield and clear the mess up."

Joe terminated the call and dropped the phone in his pocket. Across the table, Brenda raised her eyebrows.

"Ali's account of how The Mother's Ruin came into Lowfield's hands was right. And Paddy's certain that Lowfield and Manny don't cheat, and yet I got the impression from Diana that they do. Maybe George and Owen can tell us."

Brenda could not be less interested. She checked her watch. "Time to put everything to bed, including ourselves. Let's grab a quick snort in the hotel bar, then go back to Sheila."

It was a little after half past eleven when they finally returned to the Wade's apartment, where Sheila was dozing in front of the television. She had nothing to tell them, and they agreed that she would stay with Tabby for the night, but Joe and Brenda would 'babysit' while Sheila returned to her apartment to collect nightclothes and clean clothing for the following day.

Chapter Fifteen

After breakfast the following morning, while Brenda took her turn to babysit Tabby, Joe and Sheila and met with a grumpy George and Owen at a table by the pool bar.

"We didn't get in until gone four this morning," George protested.

Sheila soon put him in his place. "Well, it's a good job Brenda isn't with us, or she would have had some harsh words for you. Now be quiet and listen to what we have to say."

Taking over from her, Joe outlined the problem, and finished with his proposition. "You're the card player, Owen. Not least you reckon you are. If I can spring Ken Lowfield, how would you feel about taking him on?"

George laughed long and loud, and Owen smiled, giving them a knowing shake of the head. Taken by surprise, Joe and was not sure how to respond, until Owen lit a cigarette and explained.

"They're scammers Joe. Him and that Manny. They work as a pair and they cheat. I don't care what anyone else's told you, they're sharks. Me and George were looking for some action the first night we got in town, and that rep, Diana, put us on to a coupla clubs, and she said if we were looking for a bit of gambling, we should have a word with Ken at The Mother's Ruin. Well, we thought about it and didn't bother, but we did watch him and Manny in Manny's place. The restaurant was shut, but we could see them through the windows in that, sort of, plastic, pulldown shutter he uses. He was with them, that bloke what you were talking to on the plane, that Givens sort, and they had another punter with them. Right away, I told George what they were playing at.

Casual game of poker, no fixed dealer. Deal passes to the left after every hand. Couldn't see what Ken was up to cos he had his back to us, but I saw Manny and I spotted the scam right away."

Joe felt flustered by the information. How come Diana pointed George and Owen at the card game after she had lost so much to Lowfield? Then he remembered Ali's opinion, and he realised that George and Owen were valid punters, on whose backs she could have earned a percentage.

Ali's opinion counted for more. She assured Joe that neither Lowfield nor Manny were cheating, and Paddy McLintock backed them up, but contrast that with Owen's observation. Despite coming under George's influence most of the time, Owen was a recognised gambler in Sanford. Not only that, but he was reasonably successful, often boasting that he made enough in any year to afford the 3rd Age Club outings and other holidays. It was (so he said) one of the factors in his divorce.

Joe brought his mind back to the here and now. "So how do they work it?"

"Tell you what," Owen offered, "buy us some drinks, and I'll show you."

Joe shrugged and signalled a waiter. "Beers, is it?"

"Nope. We need whisky and water, small glasses, no ice. One for me, one for George."

Joe grumbled as he ordered the drinks. "These lessons don't come cheap, do they?"

"A lot cheaper than playing cards with Lowfield and Manny."

While they waited for the drinks to arrive, Owen dispatched George to their shared apartment, telling him to come back with a pack of cards. George promptly complained about his role as a gopher, whereupon Joe reminded him that he would get a free drink out of it, and still grumbling to himself, George left.

"You're gonna tell me they use a marked deck," Joe declared.

"Nope. Much more sneakier than that."

Sheila tutted. "You mean sneakier."

Owen frowned. "That's what I just said."

"No. You said more sneakier. The word 'more' is superfluous."

Owen looked to Joe for assistance, but their chairman shrugged.

The waiter returned with the drinks, placed soft drinks in front of Joe and Sheila, and at Owen's direction, set the two spirits, one in front of Owen, the other before George's seat.

While Joe and Sheila drank from their glasses, Owen didn't touch his other than to remove a plastic stirrer, which he dropped in the ashtray, and while they waited, he did the same with his pal's glass.

George, a big man, dressed in a pair of huge, white shorts, and a voluminous England rugby T-shirt, was bathed in sweat when he returned with the cards. "You don't need to put the kettle on to make tea. Just leave your cuppa in the sun for five minutes." He took his seat and reached for his drink.

"Leave it."

Owen's snapped command compelled George to snatch his hand away from the glass. He turned shocked and angry features on his best friend.

"Just leave it for a minute, George" Owen took the deck of cards from their cardboard pack.

He began to shuffle the cards quickly, expertly, and while he did so, he told them what was going to happen.

"We're not playing seriously, so I'll deal four hands of three cards. It doesn't matter what the cards are, because I'm only showing you what goes on. Let's just say, George and me are pulling the same scam as Ken and Manny. We're working together, but you and Sheila are the simpletons who don't know what's going on."

With a level of dexterity no one realised he possessed, he began to manipulate the cards, flicking through them, shuffling them, spreading and stacking them and offered Sheila the pack to cut. When she had done so, he made the deal. His hands moved quickly and accurately. He looked down as he was dealing, and not at the three (theoretical) players. When he had dealt all twelve cards, he placed the remainder of the deck to one side.

"Right. Because I've dealt, Sheila would open the betting, so let's say she comes in with five euros. If George has got a good hand, he'll up the ante to, say, ten euros. I don't know what Sheila has, I don't know what George has, but let's pretend I've got three aces. I'm watching you, now, Joe, and I can tell you exactly what you've got: jack of hearts, seven of diamonds, and three of clubs."

Without picking up his cards, Joe lifted the top edge of them, and his brow creased. "I thought you said the cards weren't marked."

"They're not. But with such a crap hand, if you wanna bluff, you'll match George's raise, or you'll fold. Either way, the game's cost you ten euros. The bet comes to me, and I raise again, to fifteen euros. If Sheila has a good hand, she may match or raise. If George doesn't have a good hand, he'll throw the towel in. That tells me, he's got little or nothing. By this time, Joe, you might be getting worried, so you might stack too, or maybe you'll decide to bluff again and match the fifteen euros. On my next bet, I'll go to twenty, and at that point, all three of you might decide to jack it in. If you chuck it in, you, Joe, are out-of-pocket twenty five dabs, and Sheila is down the same amount. If Sheila decides to bluff it out, she'll have to pay to call me, three aces are a solid bet, and she's lost even more money."

Owen went round the table and collected the cards, folded them back into the deck, and began to shuffle again.

"If you're in for a serious couple of hours, you let the marks win a few hands, so they make a few quid, but over the night, they might drop a hundred euros. They're on holiday. Who gives a flying one? It's all a bit of fun, and if you think about it, dropping a ton in a game of cards is a lot more fun than you lot paying out a fortune for a trip to the volcano."

"I'll stick to taking trips of the volcano, thanks." Joe modified his opinion by agreeing that for anyone who enjoyed a game of cards, losing a hundred euros in a night wouldn't be too big a sacrifice. "But you haven't told us how you do it, Owen. Those cards must be marked. How could you know what I had in my hand?"

"A shiner." He pointed at the undisturbed glass of whisky. "See, Joe, when I'm dealing, my hands move too fast for you to follow, and I dealt your cards off the bottom of the deck, and as I dealt them, I saw the reflection in my drink."

Owen, so used to playing second string to George, gestured at his undisturbed glass of whisky, and basked in the open-mouthed astonishment.

"If we were playing for real, George would be just as skilled as me at this game, and he would be memorising the cards he dealt to Sheila, while I look after you. And the signal between us is in the betting. If George folds, I know that he's dealt Sheila a good hand, and if I'm holding nothing, I won't be far behind in folding. And the same applies when I deal to you." He grinned at his best friend. "That's why you don't touch your drink, pal."

He lifted his whisky, downed it in one gulp, and George followed suit.

Joe shook his head in bewilderment. "You need a clear head and a good memory to pull that kind of stunt."

"Yep," Owen agreed. "You need to lay off the booze, to keep your wits about you, but figure this, Joe. If they're playing five or six nights a week, it's five hundred euros in the kitty, split two ways, they're pulling in two and a half hundred each. And this is Las Américas. They've got thousands of new punters here every year."

The lesson was not lost on Joe or his two companions.

"Why does Harry Givens play so often with them?" Sheila wanted to know.

Owen had no definite answer. "Maybe they play it straight with him. Happen they give him a false sense of wossname, security. They let him go home in profit one or two nights, and then clean him out over the rest of the week. He could even be in on the scam. I dunno. You'd have to ask him. But if he's not with them, and he's been playing here yonks, he'd have to be a coupla slates short of the full roof not to know what's going on."

Sheila's next objection was more grounded. "Surely this is illegal. Even here. I mean, I know these places can be a little laid-back about such practices, but I remember the 'find the peanut scammers' in Benidorm. They fleece the holidaymakers, and the local police clamp down on them all the time."

"True," Joe said. "You should see them run when the cops turn up."

Owen agreed that it was illegal. "But it's a better scam than find the peanut, because it's almost impossible to get any evidence. The only way you could do it is to put an undercover cop at the table, but Lowfield and Manny are locals. They probably know every plod on the island."

It was Joe's turn to offer something more constructive. "Five'll get you ten that they do get warnings from Vargas and his crew anyway, but with the best will in the world, the police have more to worry about than a couple of card sharks taking a few bob from punters, and Owen did suggest that they wouldn't overdo it, which makes sense. The big mistake most conmen make is getting too greedy."

Joe and Sheila left the two men in the bar area, and made their way round the pool to join Brenda. As they settled on sun loungers, Joe signalled the same waiter for fresh drinks, and looking down at Tabby's vacant lounger, asked, "Where is she?"

Brenda lifted her sunglasses and waved towards the hotel complex. "The police are here. They wanted a word with her."

Sheila frowned. "Alone? Is she up to it? I mean, the poor girl is still in shock."

Brenda let the Ray Bans fall back into place. "She didn't have much choice. I offered to go with her, but that inspector Vague Gas, or whatever he's called, wouldn't let me. I don't think they've taken her to the station. I think they're speaking to her here."

"He didn't give any hint of what it was about?"

Brenda shook her head. "He just said he had some

questions for her, and he needed to speak to her alone." She began to feel irritated. "You're the super sleuth, Joe, you go and hassle him. I'll stay here and sulk."

The other two looked around and up into the cloudless sky. Joe looked down at Brenda. "Why are you sulking?"

"Because this holiday is turning into a bigger nightmare than the time you disappeared in Palmanova."

Joe groaned. "Look after her, Sheila. I'll go see what I can find out."

He made his way around the pool, pausing occasionally to speak to the club members. Julia Staines asked him how Tabby was, and he gave a neutral reply, while Alec was more interested in the fate of Ken Lowfield, and Joe, once again, could tell them nothing. Sylvia Goodson, sheltering under one of the hotel's dark green parasols, nagged him for information, which he could not give, and Les Tanner, true to his usual form, denounced Joe as 'a pointless waste of space, even when it comes to gossip'.

At the reception desk, he asked for Tabby, and was informed that she was with the police in the manager's office. He elected to wait, and took up one of the seats by the entrance, watching some news or political magazine programme on the television. Mercifully, it was in Spanish, and to his limited Spanish vocabulary it was gobbledygook.

"Not much different to the politicians at home," he muttered to himself.

At ten minutes past eleven, Tabby and Inspector Vargas emerged from the rear office. She was white faced, obviously in shock, and the inspector left her in the capable hands of one of the receptionists.

Joe hurried to the counter. "Inspector, would it be possible for me to have a word?"

Vargas beamed upon him, displaying gleaming white teeth. "Ah, you are Señor Joe, *si*?"

"Yes. I—"

"Is good. I was wanting to speak to you. Please, come with me."

Joe asked one of the reception staff to escort Tabby back

to the poolside, where she could join Brenda and Sheila, and when that was arranged, he followed Vargas into the rear office.

For such a large hotel, it was a small, barely adequate room, the shelves lined with box files, the desk an untidy clutter of paperwork, in the centre of which, Vargas had cleared a space for his notepad.

He took the seat behind the desk, and waved Joe into a chair opposite. The previous night, Joe had the impression of a huge man, and it was born out now. In the cramped confines of this general office, he looked even larger, a huge bear of a man, a bushy moustache beneath his Roman nose, his bared arms covered in a matt of black hair.

Joe did not wait for him to lead the conversation. "You wanted to speak to me? What about?"

Vargas grinned again. "You are famous here in Tenerife, Señor Murray. Your last wife, Alison, speaks of you in the most wondrous words, and of course, we remember you from your brief visit here when you were running away from the Balearics."

Joe tutted. "It's nice to be famous, I suppose. So what can I do for you?"

Vargas rested his forearms on the desk and leaned on them. "My English is good, but a long way from precise. I have problems with the killer of this Señor Rodney Spike Wade, and I do not get answers as I should. Or if I do, I don't always understand."

Joe wondered whether to correct the misinterpretation of Rod Wade's name, and decided it was a distraction they did not need. "I was told you arrested Ken Lowfield. In fact, I saw you take him away last night."

"Señor Lowfield has been released. There is no evidence against him." Vargas became friendly and breezy. "You English, you sometimes get the wrong impression of the Spanish police. You've been watching too many of your reality shows from the Costa Blanca and Ibiza. In truth, we are no different to your British police. When we have a serious crime, we investigate, but we do not beat confessions out of suspects who are not under suspicion. Like your bobbies, we need evidence, and we have no evidence against Señor Lowfield."

Joe took in the opinion and compared it to his experiences of the Spanish mainland, the Balearics, and previous visits to the Canary Islands, and found himself largely in agreement with Vargas. By and large, the British were well behaved, but there was a significant minority who seemed to take pleasure in causing trouble, and then laying the blame on the local police for their alleged strong-arm tactics.

"You'll be pleased to know that I don't share the low opinion of you and your colleagues. You're saying Ken Lowfield didn't do it?"

"No, no, señor. I am saying we have no evidence that Señor Lowfield is involved. That is all. I do have a major problem, and it is one that I am unable to get to the bottom of, and it concerns Señor Spike Wade." Vargas's dark eyes burned into Joe. "His name, it is not Rodney Spike Wade."

Joe decided he should have cleared up the misunderstanding a few minutes earlier. "No. You see, the name Spike is a nickname. It's not his real name."

"I think I already know this, señor. What I am saying is, his name, it is not Rodney or Spike or Wade. His passport is a fake."

Joe was dumbfounded, unable to answer.

Vargas hurried on in an effort to correct himself. "Fake is not the word I mean. I cannot remember. It is false, and looks like the real thing, but is not."

Relieved that he had something he could get a handle on, Joe found his voice again. "Oh. You mean forged?"

"Si. Forged. This is the word I mean. It is a good forge, but on closer examination, it is easy to spot. Naturally, we have been in contact with the British Consulate, and they have promised to make enquiries. I do not expect to hear from them for many days, and with Señora Tabby Wade due to go home at the end of the week, I cannot wait that long. She is shocked. She assures me that she does not know what is going on. I wonder, Señor Murray, as an Englishman, someone the British holidaymakers might trust, whether you could ask questions for me?"

Joe's head was spinning. When he answered, it was almost as if he was on automatic pilot. "Leave it to me."

Chapter Sixteen

At the poolside, between bouts of uncontrollable weeping, Tabby told Sheila and Brenda what she had learned from Inspector Vargas. Both women made a stern effort to hide their shock, and instead poured sympathy upon the distraught woman.

Eventually, they persuaded her that she should join them in the hotel's interior café, where the air conditioning provided some respite from the searing heat of the morning. Brenda called at reception only to learn that Joe was with Inspector Vargas. In a whispered conversation with Sheila, she guessed that Vargas was bringing Joe up to date on what he had learned.

From there they made their way to the poolside bar, and over a cup of coffee and pastries, Tabby continued to pour out her heart.

"I couldn't believe it. It's like… It's like I've been living with a complete stranger for the last year." Through eyes sparkling with tears, she appealed to them. "Will Mr Murray be able to help?"

Sheila and Brenda exchanged a guarded glance. Joe was perfectly capable of asking questions, an undoubted success at stringing together the tiniest of logical inconsistencies, but what he knew about forged passports could probably be written on the back of a Lazy Luncheonette order note, the small squares of paper which were passed from a service counter to the kitchen, and against which Joe tallied up the daily takings.

Not that it would stop him making enquiries, and the women were fearful of the kind of business he might be getting mixed up in.

Brenda waited until Tabby had gone to the toilets before voicing her concerns. "Joe's the bees knees with your run-of-the-mill murder, but this sounds like some kind of organised crime. I'd hate to see him on a Mafia hit list."

"I think you're extrapolating matters, Brenda."

In an effort to inject a little light-heartedness into the conversation, Brenda grinned. "I've extrapolated with many a man, and it's never done me any harm in the past."

Sheila disapproved with a grimace. "We can't just laugh it off, and your silly comment doesn't fit with your concerns of a moment ago. The problem, Brenda, is that Joe's headstrong. We both know it. He won't stop to worry about the violence of a possible gang-master, will he?"

Her friend's face fell. In many ways, she was the antithesis of Joe. Where he was grumpy, she tended to the humorous. A defence mechanism, some said. She did not know, but Sheila's admonishment struck home.

"So what do we do? How do we stop him?"

Sheila had no immediate answer. As Tabby made her way back, Sheila noted just how much like Alison she looked, or rather, how Alison had looked a quarter of a century earlier. The same shapely body, topped with dark hair, and a pretty, if grim-set face.

The obvious occurred to her. "Alison."

Brenda, her mind already drifting, stepped out of her reverie. She stared around. "Where?"

"No, no. You asked how do we stop Joe getting into waters too deep for him? Back home, we could call Gemma or Howard, or even get Lee to help him, but we're not at home. So who have we here? Alison. If we've learned anything these last couple of nights, it's that she obviously has some influence over him, still, and she knows the reality of life here. She should be able to persuade him to keep his distance."

The idea appealed to Brenda, but she had reservations. "She's also involved with Ken Lowfield, even if only on the periphery because she works for him, and if he really has killed Spike, then Joe could actually end up even deeper in." As Tabby joined them, Brenda lowered her voice. "I'm thinking of thieves falling out."

Tabby took her seat and Sheila took out her phone. "I'll call Gemma."

Tabby appeared alarmed but Brenda reassured her.

"Gemma Cradock is Joe's niece. She is a detective inspector in Sanford CID."

"Yes but—"

"We're a little concerned that Joe might be getting out of his depth. If anyone can persuade him to stay away, it's Gemma." Brenda took the young woman's hand. "Whatever's going on, Tabby, it's obvious that Spike was up to something behind your back, and although Joe's the best when it comes to shoving his nose in, he's no match for serious criminals."

Tabby gave her a wan smile. "I still can't believe it. What has he been up to?"

"Who knows? Were you aware that that Givens chap is a police detective?"

"No." Shock washed across the young woman's face. "Oh, my God. What the hell was Spike playing at? And what kind of a mess am I in?"

"I don't think any of this reflects on you."

"I hope not." Tabby's lips quivered again. "All I want to do, Mrs Jump, is get on a plane and go home."

Brenda tried again. "I can understand that. So what's the problem?"

"That Inspector Vargas. He won't let me. Not yet, anyway. He says he might have more questions for me."

Alongside them, Sheila shut down the phone. "No answer from Gemma. She's probably interviewing a suspect. I've left a message to ring me back." She chewed her lip. "I just hope she rings in time to stop Joe running into trouble."

***

From the Atoll's rear office Joe considered going back to the poolside to bring up the matter with Tabby, but changed his mind, and instead stepped out of the front entrance, called at the supermarket for cigarettes, then remembered that he had bought five packs of tobacco soon after they arrived. From there, he ambled down the broad, dual carriageway to the *centro comercial*, where he took a table at what had become one of his favourite cafés, ordered a cup of coffee and sank into his gloomy thoughts.

He was so obsessed with the things he had learned that he barely remembered the half-mile walk from the hotel. At one point he passed Cyril Peck and Mavis Barker, who bid him a cheerful hello, to which he replied, "Hiya, Les, Sylvia," before going on his way oblivious to the amazed and bemused smiles from the couple.

His suspicions had been aroused from day one, but the more he thought about the events of the last four days, the deeper, more tangled, the morass became. Spike Wade, Harry Givens, Ken Lowfield, Manny Ibarra. A complicated web marinated in the thickest treacle, at the centre of which were a couple of card sharks... Or were they a triumvirate? Lowfield, Ibarra and Givens? A three-cornered band of low-level thieves, tricking unsuspecting holidaymakers out of their money?

And where did Spike's forged passport come into this? He was obviously some kind of criminal, or alternatively, someone with a criminal past and on the run, but from whom? The UK's witness protection program was a nonstarter. Anyone given a new identity under the scheme would not have a forged passport, but a genuine one, albeit in their new name.

To complicate matters further, he had seen Tabby with Harry Givens together twice. Despite the opinions of Sheila and Brenda, he remained convinced that it was them entering the Irish bar in Playa de Las Américas on Monday morning, at which time they appeared almost intimately close, and he had definitely seen them at the perfume factory in Guia de Isora, but that time, they had been anything but friendly.

He needed to speak to both, and challenging Harry Givens would not trouble him, but Tabby needed different, more tactful handling, and tact was not one of Joe Murray's finer qualities. The girl had just lost her husband – assuming they were actually married – and if he dived in with both feet, as he usually did, he could do more harm than good.

Her distress was genuine. Either that or she was an excellent actress, something which was not beyond the bounds of possibility considering her husband's deceit, but Joe rather doubted it. Even if she were RADA trained, it would be almost impossible for her to keep it up so consistently. He therefore concluded that her grief was the real thing, and he could only imagine how devastated she must be feeling this morning with the revelation of her husband's faked identity.

And yet, he needed to know the extent of her knowledge, he needed to understand how she could have been duped, he needed her to tell him of any and every out-of-the-ordinary eventuality in their life together, no matter how tiny or seemingly unimportant.

He concluded that he would need to rely upon Sheila and Brenda, but he knew the two women well enough to know that they would treat her with great tenderness, and back off from the most vital questions.

For the first time in a subsidiary career as a private investigator, Joe was confronted with an apparently intractable problem, and he was not sure which way to turn.

"Penny for them."

Alison's voice broke into his desperate, mental meanderings. He looked up into her smiling face, nodded to the empty seat next to him, and signalled for the waiter.

"Tea, coffee, something stronger, or just me?"

She chuckled. "At this time of day? I'll settle for coffee."

Joe instructed the waiter, and added a second cup for himself.

"Why so gloomy?" His ex-wife wanted to know.

"Spike Wade. Things have taken another turn this morning, and I need to handle it gently."

Over the next ten minutes, he told her of his meeting with Vargas, and the revelation of Spike's fake identity, and concluded with his problem of dealing with Tabby.

"You've got this all wrong, Joe. You don't need to handle

her gently. You don't need to handle her at all. It's a matter for the police, not you."

He reiterated Vargas's plea for him to make enquiries, but his words fell upon deaf ears.

"I don't care what Vargas has asked you to do. You're here on holiday, and none of this is any of your business. Tell Vargas to get stuffed, and enjoy the last few days of your holiday."

"You know me better than that, Ali. I never could keep my nose out."

She sighed. "It's a part of what went wrong between us. You know that, don't you?"

"We can't help what we are, girl, and you know me. People take me as I am or not at all." He rolled a cigarette and lit it. "Is Ken getting ready to reopen?"

"Tonight. Not before. Those forensic guys left a right mess in the bar." Alison checked her watch. "In fact, I'm due on at one o'clock. Extra hours to help clear up and get ready for reopening. The police haven't cleared him, you know."

"Vargas told me. They just have no evidence against him, but they'll keep on looking." Joe frowned. "Any idea where I might find Harry Givens? I mean, he practically lives in The Mother's Ruin, but now that it's shut—"

"Try Kenny's Bar. He haunted the place before Ken took The Mother's Ruin on." A thought occurred to her. "Have you tried ringing Gemma again? See if she's come up with anything on Harry Givens?"

"How did you know I rang Gemma... Oh. Brenda or Sheila told you, obviously." Joe tried to cover his laughter with a sip of coffee. "After the way she tore me apart last night, I'd feel safer ringing the Prime Minister and telling him what a mess he's making of running the country. Still, you might be right."

He took out his smartphone and dialled his niece. It rang out for a long time before finally going to the voicemail.

"Gemma, it's your favourite Uncle Joe. Things have taken another turn in Tenerife. Do us a favour, and get back to me as soon as you can. Thanks."

He killed the call, dropped the phone in his pocket and shrugged at Alison.

"A busy girl," Alison observed.

"A detective inspector now. Practically running the show in Sanford. Listen, Ali, I meant to ask, are you due back home at any time?"

"I was thinking of coming back to England just before Christmas. Only for a few days. Why?"

"Well, when you do, why not give me a ring. I can put you up, if you like." He deliberately sat back and crossed his fingers before him. "No strings. No conditions. Just somewhere to doss while you're back in Sanford."

She finished her coffee. "I'll bear it in mind, but what makes you think I'll be coming back to Sanford? It's not the only place on God's earth, you know, and I have other friends who don't live there."

Chapter Seventeen

From the Torviscas shopping centre, Joe took a taxi down into Las Américas, and climbed out opposite the Irish bar. From there, it was a short walk along the pavement before he came to Kenny's.

Notwithstanding the display of the Union Jack above the entrance, and signs proclaiming every English Premier League game live, and advertising the same live acts as could be seen at Ken Lowfield's bar, the place was smaller, more compact than The Mother's Ruin, and had about it the appearance of a European café/bar rather than a traditional English pub.

There were only a few patrons, mostly sitting on stools at the bar, but in the far corner, he found Harry Givens, poring over British tabloids. He was dressed in a pair of sensible, off-white shorts, and a Burnley FC T-shirt. His bared arms, and chubby face, were possessed of a deeper tan than Joe's; understandable, perhaps, given the number of times he allegedly visited Tenerife in any one year.

Joe secured a glass of lemonade (all he could deal with at this time of day) and without waiting for an invitation, joined him.

"Hey up, Joe. What are you doing down here? Slumming?"

Joe maintained a breezy air of friendliness. "As a matter of fact, Harry, I'm looking for you."

Givens closed the newspaper, and put it to one side. "So, what can I do you for, pal? Not looking for a bit of action with a deck of cards, are you?" He half turned and reached to his shoulder bag on the chair next to him.

Joe stopped him. "Not bloody likely. Not with a semi-pro

like you."

Givens laughed good-naturedly. "Word soon gets round on this island. Never mind. So what did you want?"

Joe ran his fingers over the outside of his glass, wiping away the condensation. He'd had plenty of time in the taxi to consider his approach, but once again the problem of diplomacy, a skill with which he had never been endowed, presented itself.

"Are you up to speed with what's been going on at the Atoll?"

"You mean young Wade? I know about it. And I know the local filth dragged Kenny in. Doesn't surprise me. A serious snapper, is Ken."

"They let him go." Joe waited to see whether the announcement produced a reaction, but it did not. "No evidence. But things got more complicated, and Inspector Vargas asked me to do some poking around."

Givens' eyebrows rose convincingly. "You'd think he'd have asked a detective."

"Like you, you mean?"

This time there was no mistaking the surprise flashing across Givens' face. "So you know."

"Yep. My ex-missus told me. She lives here."

"I remember you saying as much back in Manchester."

Joe swung the subject back on track. "As a matter of fact, Vargas did ask a detective. Me."

Studying the CID man, Joe reasoned that if Givens received any more surprises, it might precipitate a heart attack.

"You're a copper? Where are you based?"

Joe shook his head. "I'm a private eye."

"I thought you said you ran a café."

"I do. When I get some spare time, I like to shove my nose in where it doesn't concern me. I usually work for an insurance company based in Leeds, but I'm willing to bet I've also solved more murders than you. I'm known for my powers of observation, you see, Harry. I don't miss much, and I'm capable of putting all sorts of twisted explanations on some of the things I see. For instance, when I see a middle-aged man and a young, good-looking woman, going into the Irish bar further along the street, here, what's more, a man with his arm around her resting dangerously close to her... protuberances, it causes me to wonder about a fight between the middle-aged man and the woman's husband the night before."

Givens laughed, but it was obviously false; a front, designed to give the impression that he didn't care what Joe had seen or what he thought about it.

When he failed to respond, Joe pressed on.

"When I think about that fight, I start to wonder who really battered Spike Wade to death."

The smile never left Givens' face, but when he spoke there was no mistaking the underlying threat. "Do you know what I mean by slander?"

This time it was Joe who put on the throwaway air. "Do you know what I mean by people denying it, especially when there are no witnesses?" He leaned forward and lowered his voice further. "I'm doing Vargas a favour. I'm doing Tabby Wade a favour. If you won't speak to me, Harry, I'll go back to see him, and he'll be the next to question you." He leaned back again. "You see, it doesn't end with that argument in The Mother's Ruin. I saw you and Tabby again, outside the perfume shop in Guido Isadora—"

"Guia de Isora."

"Wherever." Joe shrugged off the interruption. "But that second time, she was blazing mad with you. Vargas doesn't know anything about this, because I've not told him, but he won't be impressed by your police rank. To him, you're just another pain in the backside, British holidaymaker, and you're just as likely as Ken Lowfield to have battered Wade. So why don't you cut to the chase, and tell me what the argument on Sunday night was really about?"

Once again, Givens refused to answer but Joe was not about to go away.

"The way I figure it, Tabby caught up with you at the perfume factory because she suspected that you had something to do with Spike's disappearance. Course, at that time, she didn't know he was dead, and she also didn't help —"

Givens interrupted a second time. "As a detective, you certainly notice things, but your logic needs a little attention. Are you especially skilled at putting the wrong interpretation on things?"

"It has been said."

Givens signalled to the bar, held up his glass, and at a nod from the bartender that his order was on the way, he drained his existing drink. Joe was not certain what it contained, but it looked like whisky.

A moment later, the bartender crossed the floor, delivered a fresh drink, and took away the empty.

Pushing it to one side, close to the newspaper, Givens leaned forward, mirroring Joe's attitude a few moments before.

"I can tell you exactly where I was when Spike Wade was killed."

"You must be a genius. According to Vargas, they don't know what time he died at."

"Doesn't make any difference. I had the company of a young woman all night. She'll vouch for me." He took up his drink and sipped from the glass. "What do you know about Spike and Tabitha Wade?"

"Not much. They're not long married, and they come from someplace outside Burnley. Fencing or something. I think that's about it."

"It's Fence not fencing. Let me tell you about them. I'm from Burnley, too. More than that, I'm a copper from Burnley, and I know them. She's good company, Tabby, but if you want the pleasure of her company for the day, it'll cost you €200… all-inclusive."

Joe recalled harbouring the same suspicion on Monday when he saw Givens and Tabby making for the Irish bar. "So where does Sunday's argument come in? Better than that, what about the argument you were having with them round the pool on Saturday?"

Givens smiled greedily. "Simple. When we got here, I told them who I was, I told them I wanted Tabby's company on Monday, but I wasn't willing to pay more than fifty. On Sunday afternoon, I met her in the *centro comercial*, just down the road from the Atoll, and she agreed. That wasn't good enough for Spike."

"And that's what the argument was about in the bar?"

"Spot on, my son." Smugly satisfied with himself, Givens leaned back, and took a sip from his fresh drink. "On Tuesday, she must have thought Spike had the hump on, and the silly cow followed me to Guia de Isora, and that was the argument you saw."

Joe could not tell whether Givens was telling the truth or not, but the explanation made absolute sense. He tossed the problem over in his mind for several minutes, seeking the tiny weaknesses which would allow him to attack, but he could not find anything.

"What about your pals in the police back in Burnley? If your boss finds out that you're consorting with… sex workers, you could be in serious trouble."

"As long as it's not on my own doorstep, they won't care. And the only way they'll find out is if someone like you opens their trap. Let's face it, neither of the Wades would tell them, would they? I'd nail her for soliciting, and him for pimping… If he was still alive, that is. Now why don't you do us all a favour, Sherlock Bones, and clear off before I start to get annoyed."

Joe drank the remainder of his lemonade, but made no effort to move. "You play poker regularly with Ken and Manny Ibarra, don't you?"

"Is that any of your business?"

"Not really, but I just wonder whether you're part of the scam they're pulling."

"What scam?" Givens' brow knitted. "Oh, you've been hearing the rumours about them cheating. It's nonsense."

Joe stood up. "Just shows how wrong even the police can be, doesn't it, Givens? One of my members is a card shark, and he told me exactly how they pull the scam." He grinned.

"I hope you haven't lost too much to them."

Flushed with irritation, Joe came away from Kenny's Bar, got into a taxi, and ordered the driver to take him back to the Atoll.

Givens was too long in the tooth, too experienced at this game to be browbeaten by someone like Joe. When it came to interrogation, the inspector could run rings round him. And he wasn't certain how much more progress he would make with Ken Lowfield; another hard-headed businessman, who was probably acclimatised to police visits.

As they passed through the outskirts of Las Américas, he rang Gemma again, but still there was no answer. It was strange. Normally she would respond within a couple of rings. On the other hand, perhaps it was not so strange. If she was involved in a major investigation (no matter how unlikely in a little town like Sanford) she wouldn't have time to speak to her uncle.

Gemma, and her cousin, his nephew, Lee, were the closest Joe had to children, and his relationship with both was alternately fractious (especially with Lee) and benign. For all that Gemma complained about him 'sticking his oar in', she frequently called upon him for information, not always with the blessing of her superiors, and it signified her trust in him. He did get things wrong, quite frequently, but in the long run he was right more often than not.

When he stepped into The Mother's Ruin, he learned he was not the only one in a state of irritation.

"We're shut. Come back tonight."

Alison, Mariella, and Lowfield were all busy with cleaning materials. The chairs were stacked on the tables while Lowfield ran a mop vigorously over the tiled floor, Alison was flicking a non-static duster around the walls and Mariella was busy polishing the bar.

"Why don't you take five minutes off, step outside and let's have a smoke and a chat."

The landlord glowered up from his mop. "I've had enough chat for one day. Now do like I say, and bugger off."

Joe shook his head. "Won't work, Ken. Vargas is not

convinced of your innocence, so he asked me to have a word with you."

Lowfield threw down the mop and strode towards him. Joe shrank back but was determined not to move.

"You don't listen, do you? What makes—"

"Shove it, Ken. Right now, I'm the only chance you've got of getting the cops off your back." Joe waved erratically at the far corner of the room, where Alison had paused in her cleaning, and turned to watch. "Ask Ali. She knows me, and she swears you're innocent. Talk to me. Convince me and I'll persuade Vargas."

Lowfield glanced back at Alison, who nodded. "He means it. If anyone can do it, it's Joe Murray."

Joe did not wait any longer. He stepped outside, and ensuring that he was under the canopy, out of the direct sunlight, he rolled a cigarette. He was certain that Lowfield would follow, but so long passed, that he began to have his doubts. Eventually, Lowfield appeared carrying two small beers. He sat down, slid one of the beers to Joe, then took out a cheroot and lit it.

"Before you say anything, let me tell you, I never touched that kid. All right, so there was a bit of a rumble on Sunday night, but that was it. I never saw him after I threw him out, and Vargas doesn't have a shred of evidence other than the opinion of Wade's big-mouthed wife."

Joe sipped gratefully at the beer. "God, that's like wine." He put the glass back on the table and took up Lowfield's complaint. "Vargas told me all that, but Vargas didn't know about the ruck on Sunday night, did he? And I have some minor niggles with that."

"Such as?"

"Why throw Spike out? Why not Harry? Before you answer, I'll tell you I've already spoken to Givens, and he had an interesting tale to tell me about Tabby Wade."

"Yeah, well, no matter what Harry said, he's an old friend. I had a quiet word with him later. You run a business. You know the score. I don't care what arguments my punters have between themselves, as long as they don't start them in my place."

Joe realised that he was getting nowhere – or at least, no further forward than Vargas. He switched tack. "You're sure it wasn't over one of your hooky games of poker?"

He wasn't entirely surprised when Lowfield laughed out loud. "You've been listening to the rumours, haven't you?"

"No. I've heard the rumours, true, and I've heard what Ali and Mariella had to say, but I have a different angle. One of my members is a card shark, and he spotted your game right away." Joe raked his memory. "Shiners, dealing off the bottom of the deck, you and Manny signalling to each other through your betting."

The colour drained from Lowfield's face as far as his deep tan would allow.

Joe refused to give him any respite. "It doesn't make any difference to me who you're ripping off, but I just wonder whether Harry Givens is part of your set up and whether Spike was one of the mugs."

Lowfield leaned dangerously forward. "Listen to me. I don't give a toss what you think you know. We play cards regular, me, Manny and Harry. I told you, he's an old mate, and all right, so we pull the odd scam, me and Manny, but it's only now and again, and never with Harry. He's a cop, for crying out loud. We play it straight with him, and he wins as often as he loses."

"And what about Diana? You have her telling people all sorts of crap to pull them into your hooky games."

Lowfield laughed again. "That girl is thick as a brick. I told her to keep away from you." He crushed out his cheroot. "She's my brother's daughter, you berk. I told you, I'm from Slough, she's from Maidenhead, right next door. Who do you think brought her out to the island in the first place? Who do you think got her the job as a holiday rep?" Lowfield laughed again. "Yeah, she touts for punters for me, but it's straight up."

"So why tell her to keep away from me?"

"Because thanks to Alison, I know more about you than I probably should, and I know you're not a gambler. When we play cards, Manny and I are serious. We don't look for punters playing for twenty-five pence a hand. Would you buy in at a hundred euros?"

"Not this side of hell freezing over." Flushed with confusion and embarrassment, Joe gave it up. "Okay, Ken. Let's leave it at that. For reference, I don't think you killed Spike, but I can't say the same about Givens."

Chapter Eighteen

At ten o'clock on Thursday morning José pulled away from the Torviscas Atoll, making for the motorway.

Joe and his friends had passed Wednesday evening in The Mother's Ruin where, as Alison had said, they found Diana working behind the bar, covering for Ken.

"I work here a couple of nights a week, usually when he takes some time off. Just a bit of pocket money. You know."

Joe's response was predictable. "And if I hadn't already learned that he's your uncle, what would you have told me? That you're working off your debt?"

Her pretty face turned crimson. "Oh, God. I'm sorry, Mr Murray. I—"

Joe interrupted. "I don't like people taking the mick, so do us both a favour, Diana, and keep away from me."

Throughout the evening, he reinforced the point. Whenever he went to the bar he ensured that he was served either by Alison or Mariella.

My morning, he had forgotten the incident, but as he passed through reception on his way to join the rest of the Sanford 3rd Age Club party for their round the island tour, he saw Diana carrying a large parcel into reception, and deliberately (childishly, according to Sheila) looked the other way as he passed her.

Once on the bus, instead of taking the seat behind Diana, he took the one on the other side of the aisle, behind their driver, leaving the right-hand seats for Sheila and Brenda.

Diana boarded the bus a few minutes later, and as José pulled away, she picked up the microphone and went into her routine announcement.

"Good morning everybody, and welcome to our round the

island tour. We'll start on the West Coast with a visit to Puerto Santiago, from where you'll get a fantastic view of *Acantilados de Los Gigantes*, the spectacular cliffs formed from volcanic lava. After a brief stop there, we'll push on to Icod de los Vinos, home of the famous Dragon Tree, reported to be about one thousand years old. After a stop for photographs there, we'll move on to La Orotava, a town designated as a site of national historic and artistic interest. There are plenty of cafés in the town, and we'll stop there for lunch, giving you a couple of hours to wander around the town and take in the spectacular architecture of the houses and churches, and you'll also have a reverse view of Teide from there. And when we leave La Orotava, we make our way to the far north-east of the island and the town of Candelaria, and the Basilica of the Black Madonna, an absolutely fabulous church, with some spectacular statues on the outside. We should be back at the Atoll by about half past four or five o'clock this afternoon. For the time being, just relax and enjoy the journey."

Sheila and Brenda homed in on the girl's every word, comparing her description of their itinerary with their guide books.

Joe had other matters on his mind. He paid little attention to her, and purposely forced his attention on the problem of Spike Wade's death.

After leaving The Mother's Ruin the previous day, he had returned to the Atoll where Tabby had almost become an honorary member of the 3rd Age Club. She was in the company of Sheila and Brenda, Julia Staines, Sylvia Goodson and – technically – Mavis Barker. But Mavis's attendance was no more than a technicality for the simple reason she was drunk, and sound asleep.

With Sheila's assistance, Joe took Tabby off to one side, told her of his discussions with Givens and Lowfield, and with as much tact as he could muster, told her what Givens had said regarding her 'profession'.

Joe expected her to burst into tears, but she did not. Instead, she lost her temper, and it took the combined efforts of Sheila and Brenda to calm her down.

"You've been told what the argument was about on Sunday night, Mr Murray. Givens has been giving me the glad eye ever since we arrived, and Spike had had enough of it. And as for him knowing us from Burnley, well maybe he does, but we certainly didn't know him. We met him for the first time at Manchester Airport on Saturday. If I'd known that's what he was saying about me, I wouldn't have accused Lowfield. I would have accused him instead."

"Pointless. Lowfield has an alibi and so does Givens. It's all about which alibi the police can break down, like you, my money's on Givens. But that doesn't explain how I saw you and him outside the Irish bar on Monday morning, and you looked fairly friendly."

Tabby glowered at Joe. "If you'll take my advice, Mr Murray, once you get back to Great Britain, see an optician. I never went near any Irish bar on Monday. I don't even know where it is."

Joe left the discussion there, but throughout Wednesday evening the problem continued to nag him, along with that of Diana's idiotic behaviour, and it still gave him no peace as the bus rolled along the TF-1 towards the West Coast.

Someone was lying, but who?

He had sufficient experience of this kind of crime to know what he was doing, and like any other murder it was composed of a triangle: means, motive, and opportunity. Because the time of death had not been properly established, half the population of Tenerife, including members of the 3rd Age Club, had the opportunity. Similarly, the means had not been uncovered, other than a blunt instrument. As always, motive was the most difficult to ascertain, and both Givens and Lowfield had motive, even if it remained obscure.

The problem continued to badger him throughout the half hour journey to Puerto Santiago where José parked the bus close to a viewpoint, north of the harbour, from where they had an uninterrupted view of the Los Gigantes cliffs.

His fellow passengers ooh-ed and aah-ed at the spectacular, sheer basalt formations, and Joe paid lip service to the visit, taking a series of photographs, but his mind was still on the problem of the late Spike Wade.

Givens or Lowfield, Lowfield or Givens? After a half-hour stop, and a visit to public toilets (necessary for some of the 3rd Age Club's elderly bladders) they climbed on the bus, and set off on the journey further north to Icod de los Vinos.

It seemed to Joe that his febrile mind wound in, out, and around as many hairpin bends as the shallow climb from Los Gigantes, and Spike Wade's forged passport regularly intruded into his thoughts on the choice between Givens and Lowfield. The man was obviously some kind of criminal, but which of the two potential killers, was he interested in? Lowfield: the man with questionable morals, or Givens, the senior police officer… Senior police officer gone astray?

The famed dragon tree, *El Drago Milenario*, was a recognisable icon of Tenerife to be found on a range of souvenirs, including tea towels, coaster sets, postcards, and so on. Joe had seen it on a number of visits, and was less enthusiastic than his companions as they walked from the bus, to a small park from which the tree could be seen, and from where he once again took photographs before accompanying the others back to the bus.

"You're too quiet, Joe," Brenda said. "What are you plotting?"

"I'm not. I'm thinking."

"Yes, I thought I could hear the gears grinding in your tiny mind. Is it Diana, or this business with the Wades?"

"Well, it's not Diana, is it? She's just an idiot. And what was she doing this morning while we were all on the bus?"

"Leaving a parcel in the Atoll," Sheila said. "Apparently, Ken Lowfield has an arrangement with them. He leaves parcels there, and the courier company, which collects and delivers regularly from the hotel, pick them up."

"So she's a bloody postwoman too?"

Brenda clucked irritably. "Get back to your sulk, Joe."

"You know me, Brenda. I can usually sort things out, but this is just a mass of contradictions, and I don't know who's telling the truth, who's lying, or what's next."

"And then there's Gemma," Sheila commented. "It's not like her to ignore the phone for so long. You must have really upset her, Joe."

"That's the trouble with the world today. People take the hump too quickly and usually over nothing."

It took José a further forty minutes from Icod to La Orotava, and the clock registered just after half past twelve when the bus parked on a tree-lined avenue.

Diana took the microphone. "We have a couple of hours here, and I'll leave you to wander about the town yourselves. There are plenty of shops where you can collect souvenirs, lots of cafés and restaurants where you can get a meal or a snack, and if you can be back on the bus for, say, half past two, we can be on our way again for three."

Joe, still in a semi-hypnotic trance, his mind occupied elsewhere, followed Sheila and Brenda as they took in some of the sights and expensive architecture of the town. Inevitably they visited one or two shops, and at half past one, they sat outside a café, basking in the hot sunshine.

All three opted for sandwiches and coffee, rather than a meal.

"We'll be having a full dinner later," Brenda said as she bit into a baguette filled with locally produced cheese and salad vegetables.

Joe removed most of the salad. "There was a time when I could breed like a rabbit – although I never did – and I'm damned if I'll eat like one at my time of life."

The half-jocular remark prompted a discussion on his marriage to Alison.

"How come you never had children, Joe?"

He leaned back and stared across the open square where young couples walked the footpaths hand in hand.

"It was just one of those things. I mean, I could ask the same of you, Brenda. You and Colin never had children, did you?"

Brenda's face was a mask of wistfulness. "It wasn't for the want of trying. It just never happened. You were blessed, weren't you, Sheila?"

A broad smile spread across their friend's place. "Watching the boys grow up was one of the great highlights of my life, and if I have any regrets, it's that Peter never lived long enough to see his grandchildren."

"This is it, you see," Joe said. "We talked about it, me and Alison, but we were in our mid-thirties when we married and... I don't know. What with running the café, and all the other bits and pieces of life getting in the way, it just never mattered that much. I have Lee. I know he's my nephew, but he's the closest thing I have to a son, and Danny counts as a grandson, I suppose. It's not something I worry about too much."

At that moment, Diana came round the corner, and concentrated directly on Joe. "Mr Murray—"

"Go away."

Sheila scolded him. "Don't be so rude, Joe." She focused on their courier. "What is it, Diana?"

"I've been trying to apologise and explain to Mr Murray ever since last night, but he won't let me."

Brenda indicated the empty seat next to her, inviting Diana to sit. Joe half turned away, staring again at the open square opposite.

It was enough for Sheila. "For God's sake, grow up, Joe. At least listen to what the girl has to say."

He turned back, rolled a cigarette and lit it, his angry eyes straying constantly to Diana. "Well?"

"Uncle Ken told me not to bother you, but I didn't know it was you he meant. He just said, 'give Ali's ex a miss'. Well, I thought he meant one of her ex-boyfriends from Las Américas. I didn't know he meant you. Not until later, anyway. I'm sorry. I shouldn't have bothered you."

Joe jabbed his finger into the table. "It's not bothering me that bothers me."

Brenda laughed. "If it's not bothering that bothers you, Joe, what is it that's bothering you?"

"Shut your trap." He rounded again on Diana. "You gave us a complete line of flannel. Gambling debts? Threatened with having your face altered? If you're trying to con people into a hooky game of cards, then say so. The worst I would have said is no."

Without warning, she burst into tears. "I'm sorry. Is just that people are naturally suspicious, and I had to think of a line you might fall for."

As always, a crying woman brought out the guilt in Joe. He signalled the waiter and ordered extra coffee for her.

She nodded her thanks, and went on. "I thought, you're a private detective, so you'd be into that kind of thing."

Joe's temper had not faded much. "You should try living in the real world, not some Hollywood fantasy."

"Kettle calling the pan," Brenda commented. "You should try growing up too, Joe. The girl is apologising to you, and you should accept her apology with good grace."

Joe said nothing.

Diana swallowed a mouthful of coffee. "I really am sorry." She appeared genuinely contrite. "I'm always short of money because I don't get paid much, and Uncle Ken drops me a few euros for all sorts of odd jobs. I'm behind the bar a couple of nights a week, I collect parcels for him while we're out on the bus, and I'll leave them at the Atoll for the courier to collect. And as you know, I get people to join his card schools. One thing you are wrong about is cheating. He doesn't cheat at all. Him and Manny are seriously skilled players."

Joe looked down his nose at her. "And you have my word that they do cheat."

Diana looked shocked. Brenda patted her on the arm. "We have a couple of card sharks with us, dear, and they spotted the scam right away."

Her pretty face became a mask of anger. "Wait until I see Ken. Does he know how much trouble he could get me into?"

Joe allowed himself a small, unfriendly chuckle. "Careful, Diana. You need the money, don't you?"

The bus left La Orotava at a few minutes past three, José continuing to travel north, before turning east and passing close to the northern airport. Looking out on aircraft, static, taxiing, preparing to take off, Joe recalled his frantic dash from Palmanova, making his way to Barcelona, and from there to Gran Canaria, where he caught an inter-island flight to Tenerife, which landed at this northerly airport.

It was a time of stark fear – that was the only word to describe it – but that feeling dissipated gradually after his arrival in Las Américas.

It was also, he realised, a time of renewal. By the time he returned to Great Britain, in the middle of the summer, he was back to his old self, ever determined to see justice done.

Brenda and particularly Sheila were slightly more religious than him, and when they arrived in Candelaria, they followed their fellow members on the half-kilometre walk from the bus park to the *Basilica of Our Lady of Candelaria*, where Joe opted to stay outside while Sheila and Brenda went into the church.

The seaward side of the *Plaza de la Patrona de Canarias* was lined with statues of the nine Kings who had ruled the aboriginal Guanches, and in an effort to keep his mind distracted, Joe took photographs of each in turn. By the time he returned to a bench in the middle of the square, Sheila and Brenda, looking suitably beatific, were on their way out of the church, chatting about the impressive works of art, statues and religious icons they had seen inside.

They indulged in an ice cream, Joe smoked a final cigarette, and a little after half past four, they climbed back on the bus for the last leg of their round the island journey, down the east coast, back to Playa de Las Américas.

Various delays in waiting for the passengers to return to the coach in Candelaria meant it was pushing six o'clock by the time they got back to the Atoll. Joe, for all that he had shown less interest in the tour than his compatriots, was just as tired, and his legendary irritation rose further when Pablo insisted he was wanted in the manager's office.

"It is Inspector Vargas, Señor Joe. He insists on speaking to you."

The last thing he wanted was an irritated Spanish police officer demanding progress reports, but he acquiesced, stepped through the pass door into reception, knocked on the

manager's door and walked in.
His eyes fell upon a familiar and furious face.
"Joe Murray, you're a dead man."
Joe gaped. "Gemma!"

Chapter Nineteen

The fire in Detective Inspector Gemma Cradock's eyes matched the blaze of her red hair, and the crimson glow of her freckled features.

It took Joe several seconds to get over the shock of seeing her. He dropped into a seat, and shook his head in amazement. "It's good to see you, but what in the name of steak and kidney pudding are you doing here?"

Gemma was unrepentant. "It's your bloody fault I'm here. Poking your sodding nose in where it doesn't concern you. I warned you, didn't I? Mind your own business, I said, and you wouldn't, would you? Ask about Harry Givens for me, you said, so I asked." Gemma leaned dangerously forward. "As a result of which, I've just come through a two-day interrogation with SOCA – the Serious Organised Crime Agency."

Joe's mouth fell open. "I – er – SOCA – I…" He tried to swallow but found his throat parched, and appealed to Vargas. "Inspector, is there any danger you could scrounge some coffee or preferably a soft drink from the hotel?"

With a large grin on his features, Vargas picked up the telephone and unleashed a stream of unintelligible (to Joe and Gemma alike) Spanish. He put the receiver down, and grinned again. "Is organised. Now, Señor Murray, I did not know you had called the British police."

"I didn't. That is, I didn't call the police as the police. Gemma is my niece. And I didn't know Harry Givens was wanted by SOCA."

Gemma's fury was barely abated. "Neither did I. Neither did anyone. It was so secret, I don't think the Home Secretary knew about It. I did a bit of ringing round, and the next thing

I knew, was two senior detectives from SOCA rattling on my office door. They whisked me off to London for interrogation, I wasn't even allowed to call Howard. I'm not sure that my boss knows where I am."

There was a knock on the door, and Pablo entered carrying a tray of soft drinks which he left on the corner of the desk before speaking to Vargas and then departing.

Joe picked up a glass of cola and drank from it. "You will excuse me, Inspector, but I need to clarify what's going on here." He turned to Gemma. "Tell me what you know, and then tell me what you're doing here."

Gemma, too, drank from a glass. "I'm here because thanks to you, I stumbled onto something which I'm not supposed to know about. I was seconded – without so much as a by your leave nor kiss my backside – and ordered to remain incommunicado and come out here to find out what the hell is going on. Howard doesn't know where I am, and I daren't call him, because if I do, that could be the end of my career. And it's all your bloody fault."

Joe sighed. "What is Harry Givens supposed to have done?"

She drank more cola, and took a moment to calm down and compose her thoughts.

"Drugs, that's what. He's shipping coke back to Britain, from here and other areas in mainland Europe, but no one has ever managed to pin him down. Every time they were ready to make a move on him, he was innocent as a lamb. Eventually, it dawned on them that someone was tipping him off, so they decided to send in an undercover officer; Detective Inspector Rodney Fairhurst." Her eyes bored into Joe. "You know him better as Spike Wade, and he's here with Detective Constable Tabitha Wade, Manchester CID."

For the third time, Joe was gobsmacked. "Hell's bells. And there I was thinking Harry boy was the cop."

"He was; past tense. He retired four years ago, but he's happy to let people think he's still in the service." Gemma fumed in silence. When she found her voice, she went on. "It gets more complicated. The woman you think was Wade's wife, is his police partner." She checked her watch. "In fact, I'm waiting to speak to her now. She's been out with you lot all day, hasn't she?"

Joe shook his head. "If she has, she's been well hidden." He gulped down more cola, savouring the refreshing bite on his tongue. "So much starts to make sense now: my missing camera, Spike sleeping on the settee." He concentrated again upon his niece. "So what is it you think Givens is up to?"

"It's not a big operation, Joe. Fifty, sixty grand a year, tops. We think he's importing it from here."

Joe was still slightly confused. "Why the Canary Islands?"

It was Vargas who answered. "It's very simple, Señor Murray, although it is not so simple in truth. Small boats from the African mainland will rendezvous with others out on the ocean. Some, we catch, many we do not. From Tenerife or Gran Canaria, it is not so difficult to package the merchandise with other, er, *recuerdos*... souvenirs. When it gets to your country, it is up to your people to find it. Some they find, much they do not. It is a risk that the dealers take, and I suspect that packages addressed to Señor Givens will have been intercepted on some occasions."

"Not quite true, Mr Vargas," Gemma said. "Because they never find any parcels addressed to Harry Givens. They're always addressed to someone else. He never collects in person."

"Then how did you get onto him?" Joe demanded.

"Someone grassed him up two years ago. But there was no evidence. SOCA put a watch on him, and he was an angel." She huffed out her breath. "We need to know how he's doing it, Joe. SOCA figure that Wade – to give him the name you know him by – must have got something on him, but no one knows what. Have you picked anything up?"

"No. I challenged him yesterday, but he just laughed it off." He engaged his tired mind. "We saw him with Tabby on Monday morning. Sheila, Brenda, and me. And they looked more than friendly, but we also saw them on Tuesday, and they were having a blazing argument. I wonder if Givens had realised they were coppers."

Gemma would not believe it. "I can't see it. Tabby came from Burnley originally, which is why she was chosen for the job, but Givens had retired before she signed on. She's a fast-track graduate. And no one, absolutely no one, knew about Spike. He was from Liverpool originally, now based in London."

"Was based in London," Joe reminded her. "Unfortunately, he's dead."

Gemma chewed her lip. "Yes. So Inspector Vargas has been telling me." Her brow creased. "What did you mean by your missing camera?"

Joe told her of the events at Manchester Airport the previous Saturday, and concluded, "I must have caught a picture of them shuffling through their passports, and they were worried that I might rumble them. I got the camera back, obviously, but all the images had been wiped." He grimaced. "That's one the police owe me." His face lightened again. "Why give him a forged passport? Surely these undercover johnnies could have given in the real one?"

"Too risky. His brief was to find out what Givens was playing at. If he got deep into some organised gang out here, and they got suspicious, he could bring a forged passport out to prove he was as hooky as them."

There was a knock on the door. On Vargas's instruction, it opened and Pablo ushered Tabby into the room.

She concentrated on the inspector. "You wanted to see me, Mr Vargas?"

He beamed upon her, and gestured at Gemma." Not me, senorita."

Her face took on a mask of suspicion or she stared down her nose at Gemma. "And who are you?"

"That, Constable, should be who are you, *ma'am*. DI Cradock, Sanford CID, seconded to SOCA, and I'm here to find out what the hell you and Fairhurst were playing at."

As she spoke, she took out her warrant card, and placed it on the desk. Tabby glanced at it, and the colour drained from her already pallid features.

Joe pulled up another chair, and invited her to sit, but it

was Gemma who led the conversation.

"Do you know how much trouble you're in, Constable?"

"I can only guess, ma'am."

"Inspector Vargas tells me that your partner, also your superior, was murdered a couple of days ago, and yet, no one in England has heard a word from you. Why not?"

"I was ordered to maintain complete silence, ma'am." Tabby's composure was almost gone and she appeared near to tears. "Mr Fairhurst told me almost nothing about what we were doing here, other than covert surveillance on Inspector Givens. Whenever I asked anything, he refused to answer, telling me all I had to do was follow his instructions." The first tear trickled down her cheek. "And then, suddenly, he was dead, and I didn't know what to do. Like you, I was seconded to this job, and none of my colleagues, not even my station commander know where I am or what I'm doing. So I didn't ring him, and I didn't have any contact numbers for Spike's people. They were in his phone, and Inspector Vargas has that." She turned weeping eyes on the Spanish police officer. "I asked for permission to leave the island, but you wouldn't let me. All I could do was hang on until Saturday, when I'm scheduled to fly out of here anyway."

As an explanation, Gemma found it barely acceptable. "Tell me exactly what happened."

Tabby floundered, Joe stepped in. "Hang on, Gemma. You're pushing too far and too fast, and you haven't been here. I have." He took Tabby's hand. "You had an argument with Spike on Monday night. We all heard it. And when I spoke to Harry Givens, he told me you were a prostitute. Suppose you explain all that?"

She sucked in a shuddering breath and took a few moments to calm down. "It was Spike's doing. All of it. He told me to get friendly with Givens, see what I could find out."

Joe was appalled. "He didn't order you to sleep with him, did he?"

Her tears dried with astonishing rapidity. "No he didn't, and anyway, I wouldn't have. Givens tried, obviously, but I added a few vodkas to his beer in the Irish bar. By the time we got back to the Atoll, he was drunk as a skunk. That's when I had the row with Spike. I got my hair off at him, and demanded to know just exactly what we were supposed to be doing. He told me to shut up and follow orders, I asked to speak to his superior, he told me to forget it, so I threatened to ring my boss, and that's when he said, 'I'll sink you'."

It sounded reasonable to Joe, who now concentrated on his niece. "Was he really that deep undercover?"

Gemma nodded. "Why do you think SOCA sent me here incommunicado?" She turned to Tabby. "What happened on Tuesday morning?"

The younger woman shrugged. "I woke up and Spike was gone. He'd switched his phone off, and I was worried that he might have fallen into opposition hands. I went down to the underground car park, got in the car and went looking for him at Kenny's Bar down in Las Américas. It was too early. When I came back, I confronted Lowfield, and he told me where to go. Later in the day, I caught up with Givens at the perfume factory in Guia de Isora." She nodded to Joe. "Mr Murray and his pals saw the pair of us arguing."

Joe agreed. "I did."

Tabby picked up the tale again. "I came back to the Atoll, and the next thing I knew, it was Inspector Vargas telling me that Spike was found dead in the underground car park." Without warning, she burst into tears again. "He must have been there when I went for the car."

Vargas confirmed it. "His body had been dragged into a corner where it would be difficult to see. According to our pathologist, he died sometime in the early hours of Tuesday morning, and it was a blunt instrument. Metal, painted black. That is all we can say for now."

Gemma was about to bring the interview to a close, Joe stepped in, again addressing Tabby. "Does the word *Apatedolos* mean anything to you?"

Her face was a blank. "No. Nothing. Why?"

"It's not important." He turned to Vargas. "Does it mean anything to you, Inspector?"

"It is not a word I have heard, señor. That doesn't mean the word does not exist, but I have not heard of it."

This time, Gemma did bring things to a conclusion. "All right, Constable, I want a full written report from you. No pressure, but I'd prefer it if you could get it done by tomorrow. And, just to put you right, you will not be going home on Saturday. You will stay here with me until we've made some progress on this inquiry. Understand?"

Tabby's reply was meek, subservient. "Yes, ma'am."

Throughout the debate, the disparate elements of the week's events began to coalesce in Joe's agile mind, and like a light suddenly switched on, the solution came to him. He smiled generously upon Tabby, took her hand and squeezed it encouragingly.

"Don't worry, lass, I'll sort it out. When Gemma's in a better mood, I'll speak to her. I've got her out of the doggy-do on more than one occasion. You go write your report, and we'll catch up with you later."

She returned a wan smile, got to her feet and left the room.

The moment she was gone, Gemma focused her fury on her uncle. "What are you up to…"

Joe held up a hand for silence, and instead of replying to her unfinished query, he focused on Vargas. "Do you have Spike's phone?"

The Spanish police chief shrugged. "Of course. It is at our station."

"Can you get it here? Fairly quickly? Trust me, it's vital."

Vargas looked to Gemma for guidance, and she nodded. "My uncle is a pain, but it's not often he's wrong. If he needs that phone, trust me, he's got something in mind."

Vargas capitulated. "Very well." He took out his mobile, made a quick call, and a few moments later, dropped the phone back in his shirt pocket. "The phone, it is on its way. It will be here in ten minutes. Now, Señor Murray, would you explain?"

"It's thin, but if I'm right, you'll be able to wrap everything up in the next hour. First, I need to check this phone, and then we need to bring Harry Givens, Manuel

Ibarra, Ken Lowfield and Tabby Wade here." He checked his watch. "Half past six. Can we get them here for, say, seven-fifteen?"

Again, Vargas turned to Gemma: she nodded, and he agreed. "It will be arranged."

Chapter Twenty

From the manager's office Joe hurried back to his apartment and booted up his laptop. Time was short. He had less than an hour during which he had to dig out answers to the text message, check with Owen Frickley, and examine that same text message when the phone arrived from the police station.

The gods smiled upon him. With the machine up and running, and a fresh cup of tea at hand, he opened the browser, and typed in *apatedolos*. The third entry down gave him an answer not to *apatedolos,* which produced the usual litany of fantasy handles on social media, nor even *dolos*, but to *apate*, and when he read the entry the complex tangle of Tenerife, unravelled.

At ten minutes to seven, carrying his laptop, he pressed the door buzzer on the apartment shared by George and Owen.

Clad only in a pair of humongous boxer shorts, it was George who answered. "What do you want, Joe?"

"Not you, for sure. Not dressed like that, anyway. I want to speak to Owen."

George backed off, Joe passed him, and found Owen lounging on the settee watching a well-known Hollywood thriller, originally made in English, but overdubbed in Spanish. To Joe, it was a bizarre sight. The actors' spoke, but the words, completely unintelligible to any of them, did not match the movement of their lips.

Owen greeted him breezily. "Wotcher, Joe. What can I do you for?"

"Ken Lowfield and Manny Ibarra. You reckon they cheat at cards. Everyone says different, including the cops."

Clearly offended, Owen sat up. "I don't give a hoot what they say. I know what I saw."

"Yeah, and I'm willing to go with that, but I'm just wondering if you misinterpreted what you saw." Before Owen could protest, Joe went on. "You told me there were four people in the restaurant that night. Lowfield, Manny, Harry Givens and another. Who was that other bod?"

Owen laughed. "Yeah. Like I'd know. I'll tell you what, though. That Givens sort looked like was losing a bloody fortune. He didn't have much dosh in front of him, but Lowfield and Manny had stacks."

"And the fourth player?"

Owen shrugged. "Holding his own, I reckon."

Joe thanked him, and with a nod of acknowledgement to George, hurried from the apartment, making his way back down to the manager's office, calling first at reception to ask about the parcel Diana had left with them that morning, and quoting Vargas' authority when Pablo baulked.

In the manager's office, Vargas was studying Spike Wade's phone.

"Ah, Señor Joe. I have the phone here." He handed it over. "There is not room in this office for you to speak to everyone, so I have arranged an area by the pool were my people will keep others away while you speak to them."

Joe grunted his agreement, took the phone, and accessed the text messages. To his surprise there was not one, but two. The first read *apatedolos on*, as he had seen on Sunday night, and the second, send at 19:16 on Monday evening, read, *apatedolos with you, 2 min*.

Joe cast his mind back to Monday evening, a pleasant meal with Alison, and an irritated Spike Wade on his way to The Mother's Ruin, getting halfway across the road before realising he had forgotten something.

"Gotcha."

***

As Vargas promised, an area close to the pool bar had been secured, and several of his officers stood around as a cordon, moving the inevitable spectators on, and as far as Joe was concerned, preventing those in front of him from escaping.

From the very outset, there were mutinous rumbles from Lowfield and Manuel, and especially from Harry Givens, while Tabby sat to one side, hands folded in her lap. The moment Joe arrived, Givens protested.

"What the blue bloody blazes is he doing here? I thought this was a police matter."

Gemma was not fazed. "Mr Murray is an experienced private investigator, Mr Givens, and he's been on the ground here all week."

Joe stood with her and Vargas, and smiled his superiority at the 'suspects'.

"Right from the start, everything about this business has not been what it seemed to be." He waved a flaccid hand at Lowfield and Manny. "A couple of card sharks seeking unsuspecting holidaymakers, when in fact they don't cheat at all." His next gesture took in Tabby. "A recently married woman who is anything but a wife, accused of selling herself, when in fact, she doesn't do anything of the kind." Now he pointed directly at Givens. "A man suspected of importing drugs into the UK without one shred of evidence against him. And finally, a fly guy, supposedly here with his wife, but travelling on a forged passport, which obviously makes him iffy... Except that he wasn't. He was an undercover cop. Worse than that, he was an undercover cop who managed to get himself murdered. It's been a tangle of misleading, apparently unconnected incidents." Joe laughed. "A tangle in Tenerife."

Gemma groaned. "Just get on with it, Joe."

"Sure." He took out his phone, placed it on the table before him, and surreptitiously swept his finger over the lock screen. His movements were so quick that no one seemed any the wiser, but when the lock screen – a picture of The Lazy Luncheonette – disappeared, it brought up his call records, where he had left it before locking the phone down. He began to cough, as if his COPD was playing up, and in the confusion, he jabbed the top connection, which he had installed less than an hour earlier.

A few seconds later, a phone began to ring. Givens appeared embarrassed.

"You can answer that, Harry, if you want."

The former police officer nodded his thanks, dug into his shirt pocket, and took out his phone. He studied the menu, frowned, and put the instrument to his ear. "Hello?"

Joe picked up his phone, grinned broadly, and spoke to it. "Hiya, Harry. All right?"

Realising that he had been tricked, Givens was about to throw his phone away when, at a signal from Vargas, one of the surrounding officers snatched it from him and handed it to Joe.

With an irritating air of absolute superiority, Joe smiled again. "On Sunday night, there was a barney in The Mother's Ruin, and young Spike got thumped. But during the fuss, he dropped his phone, and one of my friends picked it up. I volunteered to take it back to him, but I was drunk, and I accidentally opened the text messages. There was only one message in there, and it was sent from Spike to an unknown number." He pinned Givens with a stare of steel. "Your number, Harry. That's how I got hold of it an hour ago."

He paused a moment to let the knowledge sink into Givens' furious mind.

"It was a strange message. *Apatedolos on*. That word didn't make any sense to me, and it doesn't make any to Inspector Vargas. Over the last hour, I checked on the web, and suddenly I found exactly what it means. It's not one word. It's two. *Apate* and *Dolos*. I also found a second message on the phone which read, *apatedolos with you, 2 min* . That told me everything I needed to know." His eyes fell upon Tabby. "Spike told me that you studied Greek at university."

"I did classical studies, which included Greek mythology," she corrected him. "What of it?"

"Apate and Dolos, is what. Greek gods. Dolos, the god of deceit, and Apate, his female equivalent. Spike never sent the first message. You did. You also sent the second one, and that was your big mistake."

She dismissed his opinion. "What bloody nonsense."

Joe's accusing eyes burned into her. "Spike rumbled you, didn't he? And that's what the argument we heard on Monday evening was really about, wasn't it?"

Tabby appealed to Gemma. "Ma'am, he's talking out of his hat."

Gemma looked to her uncle. "Can you prove this, Joe?"

"I can prove that Spike didn't send that second message." He opened the message on Spike's phone, and reminded himself of the details. "It was sent at sixteen minutes past seven on Monday evening. At that time, Alison and I were sitting outside Laurel's, and I saw Spike come out of the hotel and make his way towards The Mother's Ruin. He got half way across the road and stopped and patted his pockets looking for something. Then he turned round and went back to the hotel. What was he looking for? Not likely to be his wallet, was it? Or his keys? It was his phone. He left it in the room, didn't he, Tabby?"

She shook her head. "Bull."

Joe handed Givens' phone to Vargas. "Inspector, check the call record. My guess is you will find an unidentified number in there, one which Givens has called on a number of occasions."

Vargas followed Joe's instructions, and his eyebrows rose. "You are correct, señor. There are twenty-seven separate calls to this number, some of them from three or four weeks ago."

Joe smiled. "Why don't you ring that number?"

Vargas tapped one of the records, and almost immediately, another mobile began to chirp for attention. All eyes turned on Tabby, and her face flushed with colour. She stared frantically around, leapt to her feet and ran for it. She got no further than two or three yards before Vargas' men stopped her.

Forced back to her seat, she glared murderous fury at Joe. "Has anyone ever told you what a—"

"Plenty of times," Joe interrupted before she could deliver the rest of the insult. "Spike was on to you, and he realised that he could get at Givens through you, and the one person the police never suspected of being the informer was you, and the one person we never looked at for his murder was you. You killed him, didn't you?"

Her lip curled. "Prove it."

Vargas smiled broadly. "Señor Murray does not have to prove it, señora. That is my job, and I am sure I will be able to do it."

Now she hissed at him. "It's señorita, not señora."

Gemma remained uncertain. "Why would she send the text messages, Joe?"

"Simple. An hour ago, she claimed that she didn't know why she and Spike were here, other than covert surveillance on Givens. In reality, she knew that they were looking for the full lowdown on Givens and his police informer. By sending the text messages from Spike's phone, she was trying to implicate him as the mole." Joe chuckled. "If I were you, Mr Vargas, I'd check the tools in the boot of Spike's hired car. I think you might find the murder weapon there."

"I will do so, señor." Vargas beamed upon Joe. "I must congratulate you. I would never have suspected Señorita Wade." He looked to his line of officers. "Raoul, Esteban, take—"

Joe cut him off. "Not so fast, Inspector. Tabby was the mole who fed Givens information on the police progress, but we still haven't established how Givens managed to import the stuff to the UK."

"From my point of view, that is a minor consideration. Unless you know something else."

"I do, and again it's very simple." Joe's eyes rested on Manny and Lowfield. "My good friend Owen Frickley insists that Manny and Ken are cheats. Everyone else tells me Owen has it wrong, and yet I trust Owen's judgement. He doesn't live in cloud cuckoo land. He knows what he saw: Harry Givens losing a fortune to Ken and Manny. But there was a fourth man at the table, and he was apparently holding his own."

He watched Lowfield and Manny, and from the looks of worry coming back at him, he knew he was right.

"I've had a fair bit to do this week with Ken's niece,

Diana. She is a clever girl in her own way, but she's not the brightest star in the galaxy. This morning, before we set off on the round the island tour, she left a parcel in reception, and Pablo promised to ensure that the courier collected it later today. When I asked Pablo about it, he said it was from Ken, containing local artefacts and it was for shipping to an address in – let me see if I get this right – Padiham, a little town or village not far from Burnley. I'm willing to bet that when it gets there, the Lancashire police will find it does indeed contain local artefacts, but they'll be packed full of cocaine. And when the local bod comes to collect it, they'll find he works for Harry Givens." He pinned all three men with his gaze. "That hooky poker session Owen witnessed was rigged all right, but Givens wasn't losing. He was paying for his merchandise, and the chances are that the fourth man at that table was drafted in to lend credibility to the game. He went away breaking even, or maybe a few bob in front, but if anyone asked, he could testify that Givens lost heavily."

There was an instant clamour of denials from Givens, Lowfield and Manny, but Joe rode over it.

"That's why Ken was so keen to protect Givens on Sunday night. If you'll take my advice, Mr Vargas, you'll go through Ken's bar and Manny's restaurant with a fine-toothed comb. Somewhere along the line, you'll find traces of cocaine."

"It will be done." Vargas nodded to his team. "Take them to the station."

"One moment, please, Mr Vargas." It was Gemma who interrupted. She concentrated upon Tabby. "Why?"

"You should know why. You were a DC once, weren't you? You know how much we don't get paid. Harry offered me the chance to make extra money. Not much. Another five grand a year, but it was untraceable." Tabby's angry stare settled on Joe. "Blown to hell because some nosy little sod couldn't mind his own business."

Joe did not find the remark amusing. "Five grand a year? And for that you took another man's life? If I had anything to do with it, young lady, I'd lock you up and throw the key away."

Chapter Twenty-One

As the aircraft levelled off, the seatbelt sign went out, and the captain's voice came over the PA system assuring them that they would be back on the ground in Manchester at about seven o'clock in the evening.

It had been a strange thirty-six hours since the confrontation with Tabby, Givens, Lowfield and Ibarra. Joe had managed to enjoy the last day of his holiday without anything to puzzle or annoy him, and it was made all the more pleasurable by Gemma's presence. She had spent most of Thursday night writing her report, which she faxed to her superiors, adding a line to the effect that she would not be coming home for several days, and if SOCA didn't like it, they could do the other.

"I rang Howard, told him to get himself on a plane and get down here. He'll be here on Saturday, just as you're ready for leaving."

"Good girl. You know it makes sense."

The ramifications of Spike Wade's death would reach much further than the nearest courtroom. Alison and Mariella did the best they could in The Mother's Ruin on Thursday evening, with Diana moving behind the bar to help. There was already talk of Mariella selling the bar. Joe was compelled to apologise to his ex-wife for leaving the threat of unemployment hanging over her.

"Don't worry about it, Joe. Plenty of work here, especially during the season."

As a sop to her, he treated her to a meal on Friday afternoon, and once The Mother's Ruin was closed for the night, he stayed with her, getting back to the Atoll on Saturday morning, and leaving himself just enough time to pack his case, and get ready for their departure.

Not for the first time, Alison had asked him to reconsider, and once again he refused.

"It's been great seeing you, Ali, but I don't belong here any more than you belong in Sanford."

Finally, as they waited in the airport lounge, he rang Lee, just to make sure that he still had a business in Sanford.

"It's been easy peasy, Uncle Joe," Lee reported. "Nowt's gone wrong all week. Did you have a good time in Tinny Wreath?"

"Yeah. Smashing. I've got some souvenirs for you and Cheryl and Danny."

"Did you know our Gemma's there? She went out the other day according to our Cheryl."

"Yeah, Lee. We saw her. Listen, lad, I have to go. They're calling our plane. I'll catch you on Monday morning bright and early."

The Airbus A320 lifted off a few minutes after three o'clock, and for Joe it was time to put the whole confusing business behind him.

"A Tangle in Tenerife?" Brenda said. "On Monday it'll be a tangle in The Lazy Luncheonette."

"At least that's a tangle in Yorkshire, and I know what I'm doing there."

THE END

The STAC Mystery series:

#1 The Filey Connection
#2 The I-Spy Murders
#3 A Halloween Homicide
#4 A Murder for Christmas
#5 Murder at the Murder Mystery Weekend
#6 My Deadly Valentine
#7 The Chocolate Egg Murders
#8 The Summer Wedding Murder
#9 Costa del Murder
#10 Christmas Crackers
#11 Death in Distribution
#12 A Killing in the Family
#13 A Theatrical Murder
#14 Trial by Fire
#15 Peril in Palmanova
#16 The Squire's Lodge Murders
#17 Murder at the Treasure Hunt
#18 A Cornish Killing
#19 Merry Murders Everyonee

Tales from the Lazy Luncheonette Casebook

#20 A Tangle in Tenerife

By the same author:

#1 A Case of Missing on Midthorpe
#2 A Case of Bloodshed in Benidorm

#1 The Anagramist
#2 The Frame

Fantastic Books
Great Authors

darkstroke is
an imprint of
Crooked Cat Books

- Gripping Thrillers
- Cosy Mysteries
- Romantic Chick-Lit
- Fascinating Historicals
- Exciting Fantasy
- Young Adult
- Non-Fiction

Discover us online
www.darkstroke.com

Find us on instagram:
www.instagram.com/darkstrokebooks

Printed in Great Britain
by Amazon

Printed in Great Britain
by Amazon